THOROUGHBRED

Ashleigh

STARDUST'S FOAL

CREATED BY

JOANNA CAMPBELL

WRITTEN BY

CHRIS PLATT

HarperEntertainment
An Imprint of HarperCollinsPublishers

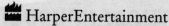 **HarperEntertainment**

An Imprint of HarperCollins*Publishers*

10 East 53rd Street, New York, NY 10022-5299

 Produced by 17th Street Productions,
an Alloy Online, Inc., company

HarperCollins books are available at special quantity discounts for
bulk purchases for sales promotions, premiums, or fund-raising. For
information please call or write: Special Markets Department, HarperCollins
Publishers Inc., 10 East 53rd Street, New York, NY 10022-5299.
Telephone: (212) 207-7528. Fax: (212) 207-7222.

ISBN 0-06-009146-0

HarperCollins®, 📖®, and HarperEntertainment™ are trademarks of
HarperCollins Publishers Inc.

Cover art © 2003 by 17th Street Productions,
an Alloy Online, Inc., company

First printing: May 2003

Printed in the United States of America

Visit HarperEntertainment on the World Wide Web at
www.harpercollins.com

❖ 10 9 8 7 6 5 4 3 2 1

"What should I name him?" eleven-year-old Ashleigh Griffen whispered to herself as she ran her hand across the swollen belly of her chestnut mare in awe.

Stardust blew through her lips and nuzzled Ashleigh's shoulder.

"You're right," Ashleigh said with a laugh. "It could be a filly. I should pick names for both."

A loud whinny sounded down the barn aisle, and Ashleigh smiled. Royal Renegade, Edgardale's stallion, called to Stardust over the top of his stall door. The previous spring Stardust had accidentally gotten in with the stallion, and now she was only a few months away from delivering his foal.

Ashleigh could hardly wait. Renegade's first crop of foals was to be born this spring, and Stardust was the first mare due. It wouldn't be pure Thoroughbred like the rest of the horses on the farm, so she'd never be able to race it. But Ashleigh knew the coming foal would be just as beautiful as the tall, leggy racers. In a few years she'd be able to break the young horse to ride; she hoped that someday she'd be able to take the horse to shows with Mona Gardner, her best friend, and Mona's Thoroughbred mare, Frisky.

"But don't worry," she said to Stardust as she ran her hand down the mare's white blaze. "I won't forget about you. You'll still get plenty of riding."

The phone trilled down the barn aisle, and Ashleigh looked out the stall door to see if anyone was going to answer it.

Elaine Griffen poked her blond head out of another stall and called to Ashleigh. "Can you get that, Ash?" she said as she forked another load of dirty bedding into the wheelbarrow. "If it's for your father or me, we'll be right there."

Ashleigh closed Stardust's door and ran down the aisle to get the phone before the answering machine picked up. It would probably be for her older sister, Caroline. At thirteen, Caro thought that painting her fingernails and talking on the phone for hours were more important than horses. She was the only member of the Griffen family who wasn't interested in racing and breeding the beautiful animals. Even Rory, her five-year-old brother, had more enthusiasm for horses than Caroline.

STARDUST IS MISSING, AND NOW ASHLEIGH'S COUSIN IS, TOO. . . .

Ashleigh dressed as quickly as she could. *Has Emily run away?* She slipped on a pair of jeans and grabbed a thick sweatshirt from her drawer. No, that was impossible. She had been so sincere the night before, when she had assured Ashleigh that they would find Stardust together.

Did Emily go out on her own to look for Stardust?

Ashleigh ran down the stairs and grabbed a doughnut off the counter. "I'm going to call Mona's house and see if she's seen Emily." Ashleigh dialed the number and counted the rings as she waited for someone to answer at the other end.

"Hello?"

The voice on the other end was so rough-sounding that Ashleigh almost hung up, thinking that she had dialed the wrong number. "Mona?" Ashleigh said in surprise.

Mona coughed several times and spoke in a strained voice. "I've got a really bad cold, Ash. My mom won't even let me get out of bed. Emily had to go saddle Frisky by herself."

"Emily borrowed Frisky?" Ashleigh was so surprised, she almost dropped the phone. Emily couldn't even ride Stardust without someone walking with her. What made her think she could ride Frisky in a storm?

As Ashleigh hurried to the phone her breath frosted the air. It was mid-March, and the wind was still brisk. She wished she could have celebrated her last few days of spring break with warm rides in the sunshine, but it wasn't to be.

When she picked up the receiver, she was surprised to hear her aunt Gayle's voice on the line. Aunt Gayle and Uncle Robert had lived out west, like her cousin Kaitlin's family, for most of their lives. But the Danielses had moved to Kentucky just over a year before. They had a daughter named Emily who was Ashleigh's age. Ashleigh didn't get to see Emily very often, since they lived in the southwestern part of the state. She felt as though she hardly knew her cousin at all.

Ashleigh and her family had gone to visit the Danielses when the family first moved to Kentucky, and the Danielses had come to Edgardale just this past summer. But Ashleigh had been gone during their stay and never got to see them. They hadn't visited lately because Uncle Robert hadn't been feeling well.

"Hi, Aunt Gayle," Ashleigh said enthusiastically. The Daniels family raised and sold Thoroughbred racers, just as the Griffens did at Edgardale. Her aunt and uncle had brought ten Thoroughbred mares with them from California when they moved to Kentucky. The first group of foals born in Kentucky would now be yearlings, and their new crop of foals would be due.

Ashleigh hoped her aunt was calling about a visit. She wanted to go see how the foals had turned out. From what she had seen of the previous year's crop, they seemed to be almost as good as Edgardale foals.

"Can I speak to your mother, Ash?" Aunt Gayle said.

Ashleigh didn't like the sound of her aunt's voice—kind of jittery, as though she had a lot of worries bothering her. Ashleigh ran to get her mother and then waited while the adults talked. She watched her mother's face go from being happy to carrying a big frown.

"What's the matter, Mom?" Ashleigh asked as soon as her mother hung up the phone.

Elaine Griffen brushed her hair off her face. Her eyes held a concerned look. "Your aunt and uncle need some help, Ash. You'd better go get your father and the rest of the family."

Ashleigh felt a knot forming in the pit of her stomach. She hadn't seen her mother this worried since Rory had broken his arm. She stuck her head into the stall that Caroline was cleaning and motioned for her to go to the barn office.

Her father was helping Jonas McIntire, Edgardale's only hired hand, unload several bags of grain from the farm's beat-up old truck. She found Rory in Moe's stall feeding the molasses-colored pony some carrots.

"Come on," Ashleigh said. "Mom's got something to say to us."

Five-year-old Rory looked up with a toothy grin, an unruly rooster tail popping off the top of his red-gold hair. "Maybe we get to go to the Kentucky Derby again this year?" he said hopefully in his small, squeaky voice.

Ashleigh shook her head and hurried him out the stall door. "I don't think it's anything like that," she cautioned. "It has something to do with Aunt Gayle and Uncle Robert, and I don't think it's good news."

They all gathered in the barn office, everyone looking nervous and confused as they silently waited to hear what was going on.

Mrs. Griffen cleared her throat. "My sister called a few minutes ago. Does everyone remember that Uncle Robert hasn't been feeling well lately?" She paused for a moment, wringing her hands. "Well, Uncle Robert has gotten worse. He's got meningitis and won't be able to work for a while. He needs to go to the hospital and get lots of rest."

"Is he going to be okay?" Ashleigh asked, cramming her hands into the pockets of her jeans. A kid at her school had contracted meningitis and had missed a lot of school because of it. She knew it was a serious illness. "What about all of their horses? Can Aunt Gayle take care of all of them by herself?"

Mrs. Griffen pressed her lips together in worry. Her husband squeezed her hand and gave her a reassuring smile. "Aunt Gayle said that things have been slipping around their farm for the last several months," Mrs. Griffen said. "Uncle Robert insisted on trying to do everything, even though he wasn't feeling well. It's finally gotten to the point that he realizes he can't keep it up. He's very ill."

Mr. Griffen rubbed his brow. "Why did Robert wait so long to ask for help?" he asked.

Mrs. Griffen shrugged. "He's a very proud man," she said with a sigh. "He didn't want to ask for help."

From her mother's tone of voice, Ashleigh couldn't tell if that was an excuse or an apology.

"He didn't want to admit that he was sick and couldn't keep up anymore," Mrs. Griffen added. "We need to make a trip down there and see what we can do to help."

Ashleigh straightened a leather halter that was hanging on the wall. "When will we go?" she asked.

Mr. Griffen put his arm around his wife's shoulders as he looked at his watch. "It's almost a six-hour drive to your aunt and uncle's farm," he said. "If we hurry, we can get our chores finished in another hour and get on the road."

Mrs. Griffen nodded. "Ashleigh, can you run and get Jonas? He'll have to handle the farm while we're gone. Caroline and Rory, you finish up your stalls and go get ready to leave."

Ashleigh went to locate the old stable hand. She

found Jonas with the broodmares and told him what was happening. Next she went to Stardust's stall and made sure the mare had enough hay and clean water to last until dinnertime. She gave her horse a hug and went to finish her own chores.

Ashleigh was glad it was Saturday and spring break. If this emergency had happened on a school night, she wouldn't have been allowed to go with her parents.

A little over an hour later the Griffens were in their car and heading down the highway. Ashleigh had brought plenty of horse magazines to keep her busy. Caroline thumbed through her fashion magazines, and Rory colored in his coloring book.

Ashleigh didn't remember falling asleep, but she woke when their car bumped down the Danielses' driveway.

Rory rubbed his eyes and stared at the new surroundings. "Wow!" he said as he pointed out the car window. "Look at how long the grass in Uncle Robert's lawn is. It's taller than our pasture!"

Ashleigh saw her parents exchange a worried look. As she glanced around her aunt and uncle's property, she began to get a funny feeling, too. Here and there boards were missing off the fences, and the horses she could see in the back pasture looked to be shaggy and underweight. Maybe she was wrong? They were a long way off. She could be mistaken about what she saw.

But when they got out of the car and walked up the steps, the broken boards on the porch and the chipped paint on the fence convinced her that things might be worse than she'd thought.

Ashleigh knocked lightly on the door. A moment later her cousin Emily's face appeared in the window. Emily had long dark hair like Ashleigh and was almost the same height. She looked more like Ashleigh's sister than Caroline did. Emily's face lit up with a smile when she saw them.

"Hi!" Emily said as she threw the door open wide.

Emily stepped aside to let the Griffens into the house. Aunt Gayle ran down the hallway to give everyone a big hug. Rory squirmed as she planted kisses on his cheeks.

"Where's Uncle Robert?" Caroline asked.

A worried frown came over Aunt Gayle's face. "He's very tired," she said. "He had to lie down for a nap. He'll be up in a few minutes." She turned to her daughter. "Emily, why don't you take the kids into the kitchen and get them something to drink, then take them down to the barn to see the horses? After we talk we'll join you."

They got sodas from the refrigerator and followed Emily down to the barn. Even though Emily was her cousin, Ashleigh really didn't know her that well. She didn't yet feel with Emily the camaraderie that she felt with her friends back home or with her cousin Kaitlin, whom she had gone to visit the past summer in Nevada.

"We might have to wait until my parents get here before we see the horses," Emily said. "They're out in the back pasture. See that black one over there?" She pointed to a black colt standing by himself. "That's my favorite. His name is Midnight Flyer. He's going to be a great racer someday. Just like the Edgardale horses."

Ashleigh saw the way Emily's eyes brightened when she talked about the black colt. She smiled, glad that her cousin seemed to like horses as much as she did. It made her feel a little closer to Emily already.

Ashleigh stared across the pasture to where a field of yearlings stood grazing on the short brown grass. The weather would be turning warmer soon, inspiring the sweet green shoots of Kentucky bluegrass to sprout.

"It's not that far to where the horses are," Ashleigh said. "We can walk out there and let them into the front pasture."

A haunted look came into Emily's eyes, and she shook her head vehemently. "No, let's wait for my parents," she said, backing away from the fence.

Ashleigh looked at her cousin in surprise. Emily almost seemed afraid.

"I . . . I don't want to get into trouble," Emily said.

Rory climbed onto the fence. "Where are your broodmares?" he asked.

Emily nodded toward the large red barn. "They're in there."

Ashleigh noticed that the barn needed a few repairs, too. "Can we see the broodmares?" she asked. "Do you have any new foals?"

Emily shrugged. "You can see them if you want. There aren't any babies yet. I'm going to go see what's taking my parents so long."

Ashleigh watched Emily walk away, wondering why her cousin wasn't anxious to show off their yearlings. If somebody came to visit Edgardale, she'd be really excited to show their horses.

They went into the barn to see the broodmares. Ashleigh noticed that the hay pile was almost gone, and the hay that was there wasn't of very good quality. She looked in on the mares, holding Rory up so he could see over the stalls.

"Why are those two mares so skinny?" Rory asked.

Ashleigh put him back on the ground. "It doesn't look like those two are in foal," she said, taking another look at the two mares. She scrunched her lips. If that was the case, that was more bad news for her aunt and uncle. Two open mares meant two fewer yearlings to sell at the fall auction, and that meant less money for the farm.

Caroline stepped close to Ashleigh and whispered, "I know I don't know as much about horses as you do,

Ash. But those mares don't look nearly as good as our horses do."

Ashleigh nodded. "They're not as fat as they should be, and they don't look like they've had much brushing," she agreed.

They heard footsteps and voices outside the barn— Emily had returned with the adults. Everyone wore a solemn expression, and Ashleigh knew that they were about to say something important.

"Kids, listen up," Mr. Griffen said as he removed his hat from his dark hair and cleared his throat. "Your uncle Robert is very sick and needs to go to the hospital for a while. Aunt Gayle is going to take him there today. You kids and your mother are going to stay here tonight while I go home and get our neighbor's big transport truck. Your aunt can't take care of all these horses by herself, and Uncle Robert won't be able to work for a while, so we're going to help out by taking their yearlings back to Edgardale for a while."

Mr. Griffen glanced at each of them. His gaze came to rest on Emily, who was standing next to her mother. "Emily will also be coming to Edgardale for a couple of months while her father recuperates."

Ashleigh glanced quickly at Emily. Her face was completely blank. She couldn't tell if her cousin was happy about this turn of events or was about to cry. Mostly she just looked surprised. Ashleigh guessed that her cousin hadn't known this was going to happen.

"What about school?" Caroline asked.

Ashleigh noticed that Emily had moved closer to her mother, and her face was beginning to fall.

Mrs. Griffen gave Emily a sympathetic smile. "We'll make arrangements for her to attend school with you, Ashleigh," she said. "Aunt Gayle will stay here to take care of the broodmares and run the farm until Uncle Robert is completely recovered."

Aunt Gayle attempted a smile, but Ashleigh could see by her furrowed brow that she was worried, especially when Emily hugged her close, her eyes full of uncertainty.

"Let's all go up to the house so you can get settled in," Aunt Gayle suggested as she rounded everyone up and directed them toward the house. "I'll be taking Robert to the hospital in a few minutes, and I know you'll want to say goodbye to him. We can get the horses ready to go tomorrow morning, when your father returns with the horse trailer."

Ashleigh hugged her father, and then they all went to say goodbye to Uncle Robert. He was sitting in his favorite reclining chair in the living room with a blanket wrapped about him. Ashleigh was surprised at how different he looked compared to the last time she had seen him. Uncle Robert was normally a robust, energetic man. But now he looked worn out and haggard, with large dark circles under his eyes and a tired look that made it clear he couldn't continue his normal routine.

They weren't allowed to hug him because of his illness, so they watched as Aunt Gayle and Mr. Griffen helped him out of the chair and down the steps to the car. They waved from the porch as Aunt Gayle headed down the driveway, following the Griffens' old car.

Ashleigh sneaked a quick glance at Emily. Her cousin stood there staring after the departing vehicles with a pinched expression on her face, as if she desperately wanted to cry but was embarrassed to do so in front of everyone.

Mrs. Griffen waved her final goodbye and turned toward the house. "Let's get dinner ready and figure out the sleeping arrangements for tonight," she suggested.

Ashleigh helped Emily dig the sleeping bags out of the closet while Mrs. Griffen and Caroline prepared supper. Rory did his part by staying out of everyone's way and watching television.

They set the sleeping bags in the living room, and Ashleigh stared out the window at the countryside. It looked a lot like Edgardale, she thought. As far as she could see, there were rolling pastures just waiting for enough sunshine to turn their usual brilliant green. White fences crisscrossed the land, and large trees provided protection for the horses from rain and the hot sun.

"You'll like it at Edgardale," Ashleigh said to Emily as she helped her pick up a stack of horse magazines from the living room floor. "I know you've only been there once, and it was only for a day, but it will be even better when you get used to staying with us."

Emily nodded as she tossed the magazines on the end table. Ashleigh could tell that her cousin didn't really want to talk about it at the moment.

"You can sleep in my room with me if you want," Emily offered.

Ashleigh could tell by the quiver in Emily's voice that she needed a friend just then. "Sure," she said, wondering how she would feel if the situation were reversed—if *her* father were going into the hospital and *she* had to go live with her aunt and uncle. She decided she'd probably be very sad and confused, just like Emily.

Maybe her cousin would cheer up if she told her about the horses at Edgardale. "My mare, Stardust, is getting ready to foal," Ashleigh said, hoping to start a conversation.

Emily's eyes lit up at the mention of Stardust and the coming foal. "You're so lucky!" she said. "Stardust is such a great horse. And now she's going to have a baby?"

Emily's eyes took on a far-off look, and Ashleigh thought she almost seemed envious.

"My parents won't let me have a horse of my own yet," Emily admitted after a moment. "They say I'm not old enough." She unrolled one of the sleeping bags and gave it a couple of good shakes to fluff it up.

"But you're the same age as me," Ashleigh said sympathetically. "That doesn't seem fair."

Emily shrugged. "Maybe when I get home from Edgardale and I've helped you take care of Stardust, I can talk to them about getting a riding horse," she said.

"With a foal on the way, right now Stardust is too big to do anything more than just walk," Ashleigh said. "But Rory's pony is fun to ride, and my best friend has a nice Thoroughbred mare that she might let us borrow. You can ride every day at Edgardale if you want."

The girls spent the rest of the night talking about horses and making big plans that included horses, horses, and more horses. As they climbed into bed, Ashleigh thought that her cousin seemed to be feeling a lot better about having to come live at Edgardale. But as she began to drift off to sleep, she heard a soft moaning sound. It startled Ashleigh out of her near-slumber. Lying in the dark, Ashleigh realized all at once what the sound was, and her heart sank. It was the sad sound of Emily crying herself to sleep.

2

Ashleigh woke when she heard somebody banging pots and pans in the kitchen. "Emily," she called as she nudged her sleeping cousin. "We've got to get up and get the horses fed so they'll be ready to go when my dad gets here." She pulled on a red shirt and grabbed her jeans. Her boots were still down by the back door.

Emily opened her eyes and blinked at the morning sun. "It's only six-thirty in the morning." She yawned. "Can't we sleep a little more?"

Ashleigh gave her cousin a good-natured whack with the pillow. "Come on, Em, there are horses to be fed and brushed. My dad will be here before noon, and I'm sure my parents will want to get an early start for home. It will take us more than six hours to get back to Edgardale pulling that big horse trailer. We've got to get everything ready."

Emily slowly dragged her legs over the side of the bed, looking as though she'd rather crawl back between the sheets and pull the covers over her head. Ashleigh felt a pang of sympathy for her. Going to Edgardale meant leaving her family and home. This would be the last time Emily would sleep in her own bed for a while. "I'll go downstairs and see what your mom's making for breakfast," she offered.

Her family was just sitting down to the breakfast table when Ashleigh entered the kitchen. Everyone was there except Emily.

Mrs. Griffen passed Ashleigh some scrambled eggs and bacon. "Dish some up for Emily, too," she said. "We need to get these horses fed and ready to haul. They've only been in a horse trailer a few times, so we might have a few problems loading them. We need to get everything done before your father gets here."

Emily came in just as the rest of them were finishing breakfast. Ashleigh decided to wait for her cousin while everyone else went down to gather the halters for the ten yearlings. Emily didn't have much of an appetite—she only finished half of her eggs and a small piece of bacon. "Let's go down to the barn," she said as she pushed back from the table. "I want to spend as much time as I can with my mom, and I want to see Midnight Flyer when they bring him in."

They ran out the door and down to the barn. The air carried a chill, but it wasn't as cold as the previous morning. Spring was definitely on its way.

Mrs. Griffen signaled the girls to join the others at the pasture gate. When they came over, she handed them the halters. "You girls stay outside the fence for now. The yearlings will probably be excited when they get turned into this pasture. I don't want any of you getting hurt."

Ashleigh and Emily climbed up on the fence for a better view.

"There's Flyer!" Emily cried excitedly, pointing to the large black yearling that bolted through the fence first and led the other yearlings on a romp across the pasture.

"Look at them go!" Ashleigh said, marveling at the leggy Thoroughbreds as they thundered across the field with their tails cocked over their backs. She glanced at Emily and noticed how happy she seemed at the moment. Emily obviously loved horses as much as she did. They were going to have great fun at Edgardale.

The young horses made several rounds of the large pasture and then trotted back to the barn with their nostrils flaring and their heads held high. Ashleigh saw the look on her mother's face before she masked it— the one that said, *Things aren't as they should be.*

When the yearlings stopped close to the fence,

Ashleigh could see for herself why her mother was concerned. The yearlings' coats were long and shaggy, and they seemed to be quite a bit underweight. She knew her aunt and uncle wouldn't purposely neglect the horses, but Uncle Robert had been so sick, and Aunt Gayle could only do so much by herself.

Ashleigh knew it took her entire family plus Jonas to take care of the same number of horses at Edgardale. It would be very difficult for her aunt and Emily to do all the work that needed to be done to maintain twenty horses in good health.

"Hand me those halters, girls," Mrs. Griffen said. "As soon as we get them haltered and tied to the fence, you girls can come in and give them a good brushing." She gave half the halters to Aunt Gayle. They busied themselves haltering all the yearlings and tying them to the fence.

Midnight Flyer was the last yearling to be haltered. He balked when they led him to the fence, but after some coaxing, he stepped forward until his nose touched the boards. Flyer stood quietly for several moments, then slowly backed until he reached the end of the lead rope. The black colt snorted and tossed his head in the air, causing the halter to snap sharply across the bridge of his nose. He immediately threw his weight backward, against the pull of the rope, and then lunged forward, pawing at the fence.

Emily cried out in fright and jumped down from the fence, running a safe distance away. Ashleigh also jumped, but she ran toward the colt, speaking softly to him, trying to settle him down.

"Easy there," she crooned as she approached the black colt. "That's a good boy," she said as she gently touched the lead rope, encouraging the colt to step forward.

Mrs. Griffen reached for Midnight Flyer and ran calming hands over his shaggy coat. The colt hesitated for a moment, then blew through his lips and worked his mouth, showing that he was thinking things through.

Ashleigh stroked the colt's muzzle, still speaking softly to him, until he seemed to forget the dangerous situation of a moment before.

"I think he'll be all right now," Mrs. Griffen said, giving the colt a pat.

Aunt Gayle wrung her hands as she watched from a short distance away. Emily stood at her side, holding on to the edge of her mother's coat. "That's our best colt," Aunt Gayle said. "We can't afford to let anything happen to him."

Mrs. Griffen smiled confidently. "Don't worry, sis. We'll get this big guy back to Edgardale and get him taken care of." She turned to the girls. "Ashleigh, you and Emily can grab that bucket of brushes and get started on these horses. When you're done, we'll give them something to eat and wait for your father to arrive."

Ashleigh turned to Emily. Her cousin was standing there with a big smile on her face.

"You were great, Ash!" Emily said excitedly. "Flyer calmed right down when you were talking to him. You were really brave to run up there when he was rearing like that."

Ashleigh shrugged. "Flyer might have gotten hurt if I hadn't." She picked up the bucket of brushes. "Come on, Em, let's get these horses ready to go." She saw a slight hesitation in Emily's face, but then the girl picked up the other set of brushes and followed her to the gate.

As they approached the gate, there was a sharp squeal as the chestnut filly closest to the gate swung her hips and took a kick at the bay gelding next to her.

"Hey!" Ashleigh hollered as she reached through the fence and gave a sharp jerk on the chestnut filly's lead rope. "Don't be so ornery," she said. The filly settled down, and Ashleigh opened the gate to enter the pen.

Emily set the brushes down outside the gate. "I . . . I forgot something that I need to pack," she said as she fidgeted with the zipper on her jacket. "I'd better get up to the house and get it taken care of so I don't forget it." She turned and walked away from the barn, calling over her shoulder, "I'll be back in just a minute."

Ashleigh watched Emily's brisk steps toward the

house with a confused frown. *Emily's nice, but she sure has some strange moments,* she thought.

Ashleigh closed the gate and started grooming the chestnut filly while her mother and Caroline began at the other end of the line with Midnight Flyer. As she brushed and curried the filly's coat, Ashleigh couldn't help but notice what a sorry state the horses were in. She looked over the top of the filly's back and met her aunt's eyes. Aunt Gayle was brushing the bay colt next to her.

Ashleigh could see how worried she was feeling. She tried to smile encouragingly. "Don't worry, Aunt Gayle," she said. "We'll take good care of Emily and these yearlings. Uncle Robert will be better soon, and everything will be back to normal."

Gayle walked to Ashleigh's side and gently squeezed her shoulder. "Thanks, Ashleigh," she said with a wan smile. "You're a good girl. I know you and Emily will have lots of fun with the horses." She moved on to the next horse and then hesitated, staring off toward the house. "Just have patience with Emily around the horses—and be extra careful," she called back.

Ashleigh nodded as she flicked the body brush across the filly's rough coat, her aunt's words echoing in her head. Aunt Gayle sounded as though she didn't have much confidence in Emily's horsemanship. But Emily had been around horses most of her life. She seemed to love them just as much as Ashleigh did. Ashleigh put the thought aside and finished the filly.

Emily returned from the house just as the last horse was being brushed. Ashleigh noticed that her cousin had changed her shirt and was now wearing one the same color as her own.

"What happened to your other shirt?" Ashleigh asked.

Emily shrugged. "Nothing," she said. "I like the one you're wearing, and I wanted to try to match it."

Ashleigh scrunched up her lips in confusion. They were going to be an awfully bright pair with all of that red. Why would Emily change? She'd looked fine in her other shirt.

Caroline and Rory stepped out of the barn. "All the hay nets are full," Caroline said. "We're ready to load as soon as Dad gets here."

They hung several hay nets on the fence for the horses to munch on while they waited for the horse trailer to arrive. By the time they double-checked everything, the big truck was rumbling up the driveway. Mr. Griffen parked the rig and stepped out to stretch his muscles. "Let me run up to the house and grab a quick bite to eat, and then we'll start loading the horses."

Ashleigh noticed the stricken look on Emily's face. Her cousin was now down to the last few minutes before she had to leave her home. Emily stuck close to her mother, and Ashleigh thought her cousin was trying to put up a brave front.

A few minutes later her father returned, and they began the loading.

Mr. Griffen untied one of the yearlings and led it to the trailer. "Elaine, I'll need you and Gayle to grab the rope and place it behind this colt's hindquarters," he said. "If he balks, just pull gently on the rope to encourage him to move forward." He turned to Ashleigh. "Ash, I want you to get a bucket of grain and stand up in the front of the trailer in a safe spot and shake the can."

"Want to help?" Ashleigh asked Emily as she went to get the can of grain.

Emily shook her head. "I'll watch from out here," she said. "I don't want to spook the horses by having too many of us in the trailer."

Ashleigh didn't think that would be a problem, but she nodded and went to do her job.

The first colt hesitated a moment, flaring his nostrils as he sniffed the inside of the trailer, but once he felt the pressure of the rope around his hindquarters, he lifted his foot and walked into the trailer, flinching a little at the loud sound his hooves made as they clattered across the trailer floor.

"Yes!" Ashleigh said as the next four yearlings loaded perfectly.

They weren't so lucky with the sixth horse. The little gray filly rolled her eyes when she was led to the back of the trailer. She balked and didn't want to move, even when the rope was pulled tight behind her.

"Ashleigh," Mrs. Griffen called, "let Caroline take over inside the trailer. We need you out here to help."

Ashleigh turned the grain can over to Caroline and went to see what she could do.

"We need you to get behind this filly and make smooching noises and wave your arms," Mrs. Griffen said. "Just make sure you're well out of kicking range," she cautioned.

It took ten minutes in all, but finally the filly loaded with a jump that landed her several feet inside the trailer.

Mr. Griffen dusted his hands on his jeans. "Let's hope that's the last difficult loader we have," he said. He turned to Ashleigh. "Ash, could you help your aunt bring up the next two yearlings?"

Ashleigh followed her aunt to where the yearlings were tied. Emily was standing outside the fence petting Midnight Flyer through the boards. They grabbed the next two horses and led them to the trailer, loading them without a problem.

When they were down to the last two yearlings, things began to go wrong. A chestnut colt that was almost as big as Flyer began to paw the ground and back away from the horse trailer. When Mr. Griffen pressured him, the colt rose into the air, pawing the air and slinging his head from side to side.

Mr. Griffen tightened his hold and shouted instructions to the women. When the chestnut kicked out against the rope that was against his hindquarters, Ashleigh saw her mother and Aunt Gayle scatter.

Midnight Flyer began to toss his head and snort. Ashleigh gave a warning tug on the rope and the colt settled down, but the chestnut continued his shenanigans. The horses in the trailer called out in fright and pawed at the floor. "Easy," Ashleigh said, but she could tell things were quickly getting out of hand. She needed to get into the trailer and calm down the nervous yearlings. "Emily, come here!" Ashleigh cried. "Hold Flyer while I help with the other yearlings," she said as she tossed the lead rope to her cousin.

Emily started to protest, but Ashleigh gave her a reassuring nod and ran to the horse trailer. She entered the rig and spoke softly to the colts and fillies while her parents and aunt got the chestnut back under control. The yearlings nickered to each other and called to the horses outside the trailer.

Ashleigh heard Emily shout her name. She turned to peek out of the trailer and saw Flyer tossing his head and pawing at the ground. "Give him a tug on the rope," Ashleigh yelled. She heard the thump of hooves on the trailer floor and knew that the chestnut had been loaded.

"Ashleigh!" Emily called in a frightened voice.

Ashleigh stepped from the trailer to see what was troubling her cousin. As Flyer snorted impatiently and jerked his head, Emily jumped away from the black colt and dropped the lead rope with a frightened squeal.

Flyer immediately knew he was free. He reared and struck at the air, then whirled in a cloud of dust and sprinted away, his long black mane and tail floating on the breeze.

"Somebody cut him off!" Mr. Griffen yelled.

But it was too late. Flyer ducked around the line of people and pounded down the driveway. Everyone watched in shock as the valuable yearling headed toward the busy road.

3

Everyone hesitated, too surprised to move. Then Ashleigh, her parents, her sister, and her aunt all moved at once, running furiously down the driveway behind the black colt. Ashleigh knew that all of their efforts were futile. They could never catch up to Flyer on foot. Their only hope was that he would change his mind and stop before he got down to the road.

Ashleigh saw her father slow down. He put his hand up, motioning for them all to stop. She halted beside him, feeling her lungs burn as she gulped in big breaths of air.

"We're just driving him on," Mr. Griffen said.

They stood helplessly watching the colt's headlong flight toward the road.

"Oh, no!" Ashleigh cried as she gripped her father's arm, pointing to the big truck that was roaring down the road, oblivious to the speeding Thoroughbred colt. She held her breath, hoping for a miracle. "Come on, Flyer," she begged in a whisper. "Turn around, boy, please."

But the black colt continued his flight, on a collision course with the oncoming truck. Ashleigh jumped as the truck driver blared his horn, but Flyer galloped onto the road, his hooves beating a rapid tattoo as he charged across the two-lane highway. Ashleigh sucked in her breath, wanting to close her eyes to the accident that was about to occur, but she was unable to turn away.

There was a screech of brakes and smoke flew from the tires as the truck driver tried to avoid hitting the colt. Flyer's ears flicked in the direction of the noise as he sped across the pavement, pouring on more speed and narrowly missing the large vehicle.

Ashleigh's breath came out in a whoosh when Flyer reached the other side of the road unharmed. He galloped over to a fence where several other horses stood.

Everyone let out a huge sigh of relief.

"Let's go get him before he decides to come back across the road," Elaine Griffen said.

They looked both ways to make sure there were no cars, then sprinted across the highway to where Midnight Flyer stood trading squeals and snorts with the other horses.

"Easy, Flyer," Mr. Griffen said as he moved slowly up

to the colt. "Got him!" he said, buckling the strap on the halter and gripping the lead rope firmly.

Ashleigh let out a big sigh of relief. Flyer was safe. She fell into step beside her father as he led the colt back to the trailer.

Emily and Rory were waiting for them when they returned, Emily kicking at the dirt and biting her lip. Her face lit with pure relief when she saw that Midnight Flyer was all right. Ashleigh joined her while the adults loaded the spirited colt into the trailer.

"You're incredibly brave!" Emily said as she gave Ashleigh a quick hug. "I'm so glad Flyer is safe. Thank you so much!"

Ashleigh's cheeks colored. She hadn't really done anything except run after the colt. It was only luck or fate that had gotten the colt safely across the road. She shifted from foot to foot. The admiring look she saw in her cousin's eyes made her a little uncomfortable. "What happened, Em?" Ashleigh asked, trying to keep the question from sounding like an accusation. Flyer hadn't been acting that badly. As far as Ashleigh could tell, there hadn't been any reason for Emily to let go of his lead.

Emily lowered her chin and shrugged. "It doesn't matter," she said as she kicked at the dirt with the toe of her shoe. "Flyer is safe, thanks to you and your parents."

Ashleigh frowned. "But it does matter!" she blurted out as she stared in confusion at Emily. "Flyer could have been hit by that truck! He's the best horse you've got, and he almost got killed because you turned him loose!"

Ashleigh saw the tears welling up in her cousin's eyes, and suddenly she felt like a bully. A moment later, when the first tear slid down Emily's cheek, she felt even worse.

Emily quickly jammed her hands into her pockets and turned away from Ashleigh.

Ashleigh could see her cousin's shoulders shake with sobs. Her heart sank. She had made Emily cry. "It's okay, Em," she said, awkwardly patting Emily's back.

Emily turned toward Ashleigh, her face wet with tears. "It's *not* okay," she sobbed as she balled her fists at her sides. "I know it's my fault that Flyer got loose. He could have been killed because I'm a big chicken!" She swiped her hand angrily across her face. "I'm not brave like you, Ash," Emily admitted. "I'm afraid of horses."

Ashleigh's jaw dropped open, then snapped shut. *Emily's afraid of horses?* "What do you mean?" she said, thinking of all the big plans they had made to work with the horses at Edgardale. Why had Emily agreed to do all of those things if she was afraid of horses?

"I used to be like you, Ash," Emily said as she brushed away another trail of tears. "I could be around horses all the time and never be afraid." She stared out over the distant fields and sighed. "I had a pony of my own, and I used to ride him everywhere. After he died, I asked my parents if I could get a horse, but they thought I was too young. Money was kind of tight, so they asked me to wait a year, but I didn't want to."

Caroline popped her head around the corner of the trailer with a questioning look on her face. Ashleigh waved her off and walked Emily toward the barn, away from everyone, so they could talk in private. She was sure Emily wouldn't want everyone to know she was crying.

Emily sat on a bale of straw in the barn aisle. "I didn't want to wait an entire year," she repeated. "A year sounds like forever when you've been riding almost every day."

Ashleigh nodded and smiled. She knew exactly what her cousin meant. She missed being able to canter Stardust over the fields.

"Anyway," Emily said as she pulled a piece of straw from the bale and began shredding it, "we have a broodmare named Chloe that I really like, and she's always been really easy to handle. I thought she'd make a good riding horse for me during her first months of pregnancy. I asked my parents, but they said no. They thought Chloe was too much horse for me." She looked Ashleigh in the eye. "But I didn't believe them, so I rode her anyway."

Ashleigh leaned forward, anxious to hear the end of the story. "What happened?"

Emily rolled up her sleeve, exposing her elbow for Ashleigh's inspection. "They tell me I got this when I got bucked off," she said. "I don't remember it, though. I remember galloping across the pasture, and Chloe kept going faster and faster. I couldn't stop her. Then she started bucking, and I flew through the air." Emily took a deep breath and let it out slowly. "All I remember is hitting the ground, then coming to and feeling like my whole body was one big bucket of pain."

"Wow," Ashleigh said, tracing the two-inch-long scar on her cousin's elbow. "Did you break anything?"

Emily nodded. "I cracked a couple of ribs, and I had a concussion. I'm not sure how long I lay there unconscious, but my mom found me and took me to the hospital. Ever since then, I've been afraid of horses."

Ashleigh gave Emily an encouraging smile. "Don't worry, Em. I'll help you get back to working with horses again. Stardust is really gentle. She'd be a good horse for you to start with."

The truck's horn blared, signaling that her father was ready to pull out. Ashleigh saw the stricken look on Emily's face. It was time for her cousin to leave her parents and her home and come to live with them at Edgardale for a while. "Go say goodbye to your mom," she said softly. "We'll ride with my father in the horse rig. I'll see you there in a few minutes."

Ashleigh climbed into the tall truck and watched as Emily hugged her mother. She hoped she'd be able to help her cousin get adjusted to life at Edgardale.

A few minutes later Emily climbed into the truck and fastened her seat belt. She dragged the back of her hand over her eyes and gave one loud sniff, then turned to Ashleigh with a tremulous smile. "I'll be all right," she reassured her. "My mom promised to call every night and visit when she can. We're going to have a great time at Edgardale. Maybe I'll even be able to ride again by the time I go home."

"I guarantee it," Ashleigh said confidently.

Emily slept most of the way home. Ashleigh felt sleepy, too, but she busied herself with the horse magazines she'd meant to read on the ride over. She woke Emily when they pulled into Edgardale's long gravel driveway.

Ashleigh noticed that despite some chilly March days, the trees were beginning to bud. Soon new green leaves would cover the trees and flowers would begin to poke from the rich Kentucky dirt.

Several of their broodmares were expected to foal soon. A smile stole across Ashleigh's lips. One of them was Stardust. In just a few weeks she'd be saying hello to Stardust's perfect foal!

The truck rumbled into the barnyard, and Mr. Griffen braked to a stop. "Here we are," he said as he opened the truck's door and jumped to the ground. "Emily, Rory, and Caroline will take you up to the house and show you around. Ashleigh will be up as soon as we get these horses settled."

Ashleigh shot Emily an encouraging glance, then ran into the barn to make sure all the stalls were properly prepared.

Jonas appeared around the corner. He settled his hat on his graying head and nodded toward the horse trailer. "I'll help your parents unload," he said as he strode toward the door. "You make sure the stall doors are open as we bring each of the yearlings in."

They quickly got all of the horses settled into their new stalls. Ashleigh noticed that a couple of the colts had runny noses. She made a mental note to keep Stardust away from them. She didn't want her mare getting sick and endangering the foal.

When they finished, Ashleigh and her parents returned to the house. They were greeted with the sight of Emily sitting on the couch with tears streaming down her face, her shoulders shaking with sobs. Rory perched on the end of the couch, looking nervous and sympathetic, and Caroline sat next to Emily with her arm around the girl, trying to console her.

Mrs. Griffen quickly wiped her boots and strode into the living room. "What's the matter, Em?" she asked in concern as she knelt in front of Emily.

Emily didn't speak immediately, so Caroline spoke for her. "She's a little disappointed with the room arrangements," she said, rubbing Emily's back in sympathy.

Emily nodded in agreement, her eyes still on the floor.

Mrs. Griffen brushed back Emily's dark bangs from her forehead. "I'm sorry, honey. I moved you into Rory's room because I thought you were used to having a room by yourself and might like it that way."

Emily shook her head. "I . . . I'd rather be in Ashleigh's room." She sniffed, drawing herself up straighter.

"I can move into Rory's room while Emily is here," Caroline volunteered. "Emily can have my bed if it makes her feel better." She turned to Ashleigh and whispered, "Remember, Ash, Emily has just left her parents and she's in a strange place. We need to be extra nice to her."

Ashleigh pursed her lips. She thought her family was already being as nice to Emily as they could. But if moving into Caroline's bed made her cousin feel better, it wouldn't hurt anything.

Emily smiled weakly at this news and seemed to quickly recover from her tears. With the room arrangements settled, Ashleigh went to help Emily transfer her things to Caroline's side of the room. Emily perked up a little and chatted with Ashleigh as she unpacked her suitcase. It seemed as though she had totally forgotten the incident that had taken place just moments before.

It took them a while to unpack, and by the time they were done, Ashleigh could smell the delicious scent of lasagna drifting up the stairs from the kitchen. Ashleigh looked at the blotches of dirt on the shirt she'd worn to haul the horses. She knew her mother would send her right back to change if she showed up at the dinner table wearing it. She grabbed a blue pullover from her closet and quickly changed, then sat on the corner of her bed and braided her hair into one thick strand that hung down her back. "I need to go down and help Caroline set the dinner table," Ashleigh told her cousin. "I'll see you downstairs in a few minutes, okay?"

Emily wiped her nose and nodded with a smile. "Okay, Ashleigh."

Ashleigh felt herself smiling back. Maybe her cousin would be happy at Edgardale after all.

Downstairs Caroline handed Ashleigh a stack of plates, and they set the table together while their mother pulled the lasagna from the oven.

"Mmm," Ashleigh said, taking a big sniff of the yummy-looking dish. "I'm so hungry, I could eat the whole pan."

Rory furrowed his brow. "Save me a piece, Ash. You can't eat it all."

Ashleigh ruffled Rory's hair as the rest of the family laughed. "I was only joking, Rory," she said with a grin. "I'd never get to be a jockey if I went around eating entire pans of lasagna."

Emily came down the stairs just as everyone was getting seated. She gave the Griffens a big smile and took the chair next to Ashleigh. Ashleigh wanted to smile back, but Emily's appearance left her staring in disbelief. Emily had changed into a blue pullover and wore a single braid down her back, just like Ashleigh!

Rory's brows rose as he studied the two girls. "You guys looks like twins," he observed as he glanced from Ashleigh to Emily. "Emily's shirt is a little darker blue, but your hair is just the same."

Emily looked pleased, but Ashleigh frowned. Why was Emily trying to copy her? This was the second time her cousin had dressed just like her, and Ashleigh wasn't at all sure that she liked it. Her family had insisted that everyone try to make Emily's stay as fun as possible. But Ashleigh was beginning to wonder how much fun Emily's visit would be for *her*.

4

Ashleigh's appetite was suddenly gone. Why was Emily so unpredictable? One moment they were making plans to do fun horse things, and Ashleigh thought they would have a great time together. But then Emily would go and do something stupid, such as be a copy-cat or admit that she was afraid of horses.

As she contemplated recent events, Ashleigh forked a bite of lasagna and blew on it before popping it into her mouth. When the tangy taste of tomato and rich melted cheese reached her taste buds, she momentarily forgot about her problems with Emily.

Mrs. Griffen passed the tossed salad to Emily. "I think we should discuss what will be expected of you while you're here, Emily," she said. "Your schedule probably won't be much different than it was at home. You'll get up with the rest of the kids and do your share of barn chores before breakfast. There'll be a few more

39

chores after school, and then your time is your own." She offered Emily the plate of garlic bread. "You'll be expected to have all of your homework finished before bedtime."

"Will I be handling the horses?" Emily asked.

Ashleigh saw the worried look that entered her cousin's eyes. Her parents didn't know that Emily was afraid of horses. Her cousin seemed to be embarrassed about being afraid, otherwise she would have told the rest of the family, too. Ashleigh took another big bite of the pasta. That secret would be hard to keep on a horse farm. And if Emily didn't tell her parents soon, she might end up putting another horse in danger.

After dinner Ashleigh made a quick trip to the barn to make sure Stardust was all right. She rubbed the mare's neck and told her about her strange cousin. "She wants to be able to work with horses again without being afraid," Ashleigh told the little chestnut mare. "But I think it's going to be really hard for her. You'll have to help us out and be on your best behavior when Emily is around."

Stardust nuzzled Ashleigh's shoulder as if they were making a pact.

"I knew I could count on you, girl," Ashleigh said with a smile. She kissed the mare on the tip of the nose and patted her good night, then went back to the house.

Emily was already making herself at home when

Ashleigh entered her room. All of her clothes were put neatly in the drawers, and she was lining up her horse magazines beside Ashleigh's.

Ashleigh opened her closet and studied her clothes, deciding what to wear the following day. She laid out a lightweight brown sweater and cringed when she saw Emily pull out a brown shirt that was almost the same color as the sweater she had just chosen.

"Maybe you should wear the blue one," Ashleigh suggested. "That's a good color on you. You'll want to make a good impression on your first day at this school."

Emily shook her head. "Nope," she said cheerfully, holding up the brown shirt. "This is definitely the one I'm going to wear."

Ashleigh considered changing her mind and picking a new shirt, but she decided that Emily would probably do the same. And she didn't really want to get into a fight with Emily. She didn't want to make her feel awkward on her first night at Edgardale.

They busied themselves in silence for several moments, and then Emily began to ask questions about school. Ashleigh filled her in on all the details, even telling her about the new boy who had just moved in down the road.

"No one has seen him yet, but I hear his name is Justin. He's supposed to be starting school tomorrow, too," Ashleigh said. "Mona heard that his family raises and races Thoroughbreds, so we'll have to make sure we get to know him. He might be fun to have as a friend."

Emily nodded excitedly. "There aren't very many kids my age where we live," she said. "It's going to be fun to have so many friends here." She picked up one of Ashleigh's horse magazines and thumbed through it. "Especially when they all love horses," she said.

Ashleigh gathered up her pajamas and padded to the bathroom. "Better get ready for bed, Em," she called over her shoulder as she clicked on the bathroom light. "Six o'clock is going to feel awfully early tomorrow."

But Emily didn't take Ashleigh's advice. Long after Ashleigh had finished her bedtime preparations and snuggled under the covers, Emily stayed up, looking through all of Ashleigh's horse magazines. Ashleigh's mother poked her head in and gave a five-minute warning on the lights, but Emily found the flashlight in the nightstand and was still reading when Ashleigh dropped off to sleep.

"Come on, Em, it's time to get up." Ash gave her cousin a good shake and then reached for her barn clothes. Stardust was surely waiting for her breakfast. Ashleigh had to mix a lot of vitamins and wheat germ oil into the mare's grain, just as they did with the other broodmares, so that she would deliver a healthy foal. Althea and My Georgina, bred by another Edgardale stallion, were due to foal any minute. There were only a few Edgardale mares bred to Renegade, because he had started breeding very late in the season.

Emily groaned and rolled onto her side. "I don't feel very good," she grumbled.

Ashleigh could barely make out her cousin's form in the weak dawn light. She stuck her arms into the sleeves of her sweatshirt, pulling the warm garment over her head. "What's the matter, Em?" she asked as her head popped through the neck hole, making her long dark hair crackle with static electricity in the cool morning air.

"My stomach hurts," Emily moaned.

Ashleigh tiptoed to the door. "I'll let you sleep a little more," she said. "I'll do your chores this morning." She closed the door with a soft click. *Poor Emily probably is nervous about her first day at a new school,* Ashleigh thought.

Her mother was making pancakes as Ashleigh slipped through the kitchen on her way to the barn. "Emily's not feeling well this morning," Ashleigh said, pulling on her boots. "I'll do her chores. If she sleeps a little longer, maybe she'll feel good enough to go to school."

"That's nice of you, Ash," Mrs. Griffen said as she flipped a golden brown pancake onto a plate, then put it in the oven to warm until everyone was ready for breakfast. "I'll go up and check on her in a little while."

Ashleigh heard voices coming from the foaling stall when she entered the barn. Had one of the mares foaled during the night? She quickened her steps, grinning as she heard the high-pitched whinny of a newborn foal and the answering nicker of its dam.

She poked her head over the door to see her father and Jonas putting iodine on the new filly's umbilical cord while a nervous Althea watched the proceedings from the corner of the stall.

Ashleigh smiled dreamily as she watched the tiny filly shuffle unsteadily to her mother and begin to suckle. Stardust's foal would probably look similar to this one, she thought. She hoped it would have the long legs and elegant body of a Thoroughbred, and the beautiful white blaze that Stardust had.

"What do you think of our first foal of the season?" Mr. Griffen asked with a smile. He passed the bottle of iodine to Jonas and got to his feet, dusting his hands on his pants.

"She's beautiful!" Ashleigh cried. "If I do my chores quickly, can I handle her some before breakfast?"

All of Edgardale's foals were handled from birth. Ashleigh knew that her father and Jonas would have imprinted the new filly not long after it emerged. Imprinting consisted of rubbing the foal's entire body, including the inside of its ears and mouth, to get it used to humans and to being handled. That was one of Ashleigh's favorite things at foaling time. It made the new ones more trustful of humans, and it helped them to be kinder horses that were easy to handle as they grew up.

"Where's Emily this morning?" Mr. Griffen asked as he and Jonas left the stall.

Ashleigh followed them to the feed room, grabbing the buckets that were stacked in the corner. "She doesn't feel very well," she answered, debating whether to tell her father about Emily's late-night reading. She decided to keep quiet about it. After all, there had been plenty of nights when she herself had stayed up past bedtime to finish a new issue of one of her favorite magazines. "I told her I'd do her chores this morning. I figured that if she got a little extra rest, she'd feel better."

A half hour later, when Ashleigh entered the house behind Rory and Caroline, she was surprised to see Emily sitting at the table with a large stack of pancakes in front of her. Ashleigh furrowed her brow. It looked as though Emily's stomachache was gone.

She pulled up a chair and lifted two pancakes from the platter in the middle of the table, covering them with rich, gooey maple syrup before cutting them into bite-sized morsels and popping them into her mouth. From the corner of her eye, Ashleigh watched Emily devour the entire plateful of pancakes. She couldn't help thinking she had been duped into doing her cousin's chores. She promised herself that Emily wouldn't fool her again.

Mrs. Griffen poured herself a hot cup of coffee, setting one in front of her husband, too. "You kids had better hurry and change into your school clothes. The bus will be here in ten minutes."

Ashleigh finished her breakfast and ran upstairs to wash up and get ready for school. She waited until the last second to put on her fresh clothes. When her mother shouted up the stairs that she was going to be late, Ashleigh hung her brown sweater back in the closet and pulled out one that was forest green. She felt a little guilty about tricking Emily in the clothes game, but it served her cousin right for allowing Ashleigh to do her morning chores when she wasn't really sick. Besides, Emily already looked enough like Ashleigh. She didn't want the kids at school teasing them for dressing alike.

She ran down the stairs and grabbed her book bag off the counter before rushing out the door to join Caroline and Emily for the walk down the long driveway.

Ashleigh's coat was unzipped a few inches, and she saw Emily's brows knit when she realized that Ashleigh had changed her shirt. Ashleigh tried to act as though she hadn't noticed, and continued down the driveway. They weren't going to be twins that day.

Mona was waiting for them at the bus stop, her hands shoved deep into the pockets of her coat to fend off the morning chill. It was supposed to climb to seventy degrees by the end of the day, but for now they could see their own breath as they trudged toward the bus stop.

Ashleigh made the introductions, and Emily immediately started chatting, asking Mona all about her horse. Ashleigh wanted to ask her friend if she had heard anything more about the new boy, but Emily wouldn't let her get a word in edgewise.

Caroline's bus was the first to arrive, but the bus for the middle school was not far behind it. When the big yellow bus screeched to a stop, Ashleigh got in line behind Mona and Emily, expecting to take her usual seat beside her best friend. But Emily plopped right into the double seat next to Mona, leaving Ashleigh to sit with the school bully several rows back.

She crammed her books under the seat in front of her, trying to ignore the big kid who was trying to get a rise out of her by pulling on her hair. Ashleigh closed her eyes and sighed. It was going to be a long, exasperating day.

5

By the time the bus pulled onto the school grounds, Ashleigh was ready to scream. She took a deep, calming breath, reminding herself that Emily was new and it was only natural that she would want to make friends. Ashleigh just wished her cousin would make friends of her own. She didn't want to have to share all of Mona's time with Emily.

She grabbed her book bag and stood to exit the bus, slapping away the bully's hand when he reached for her hair one last time. She shuffled off the bus quickly and joined Mona and Emily outside on the sidewalk.

"I have to take Emily to the office," Ashleigh said to Mona as she pulled open the brick schoolhouse's heavy front door. "I'll see you in class."

She walked Emily down the long hall covered with bulletin boards that held announcements and colorful artwork created by her classmates. When they reached the office, there was a boy waiting at the counter whom Ashleigh didn't recognize. She was pleasantly surprised to find out that it was the new boy who had moved in down the road from Edgardale. The school secretary introduced him as Justin Smith. Both he and Emily were going to be in several of Ashleigh's classes, so she walked them to their first-period classroom.

Justin was a red-haired boy who was several inches taller than Ashleigh. He had a long, flowing stride, just like the lanky Thoroughbreds they raised at Edgardale. He was very polite, and Ashleigh immediately took a liking to him.

Mrs. Wilson, their teacher, assigned Emily to sit on one side of Ashleigh, with Justin taking the seat on the other side.

"Ashleigh, would you please introduce our two new students to the class?" Mrs. Johnson asked.

Ashleigh felt rather awkward having to stand up in front of everybody, but at least she got to sit down as soon as she had performed the task. Emily and Justin had to remain standing while they told the other students something about themselves.

Justin explained that he and his family had just moved from their farm in upstate New York, where they'd raised and trained racehorses. His family was hoping to break into the big time at Churchill Downs.

"We've got a two-year-old colt that's really amazing," Justin said. "My parents plan to start Fancy Cat this fall. If he runs well, we'll point him toward the Derby next year as a three-year-old."

Justin sat down, and all eyes turned to Emily. For a moment Ashleigh wasn't sure if she was going to speak. Her cousin looked kind of blank, like a deer caught in the headlights. Ashleigh nodded encouragingly, and Emily hesitatingly began to talk.

"My name is Emily, and I'm here staying with my cousin Ashleigh for a few months because my dad is recovering from an illness. My family raises racehorses, just like Ashleigh's and Justin's do." She stopped and gave Justin a big smile. "My family's Thoroughbred yearlings came to live at Edgardale with me. Ashleigh and I are going to work with them."

With that, Emily sat back in her chair, and Ashleigh thought her cousin looked a little sad. It must have been hard to be reminded that she was away from home and worried about her ailing father.

The rest of the morning's classes passed quickly, except for math, which Ashleigh always had trouble with, and before long they were heading for the lunchroom.

Ashleigh handed a tray to Emily and one to Mona. "It looks like meatloaf day again," she said. "Yuck!"

Emily gathered her silverware and a napkin. "I like meatloaf. I'll eat yours, too, if you don't want it."

Mona grabbed the plate that the cafeteria helper handed her. She set it on her tray and wrinkled her nose. "You won't like *this* meatloaf," she warned. "But at least they've got mashed potatoes, green beans, and cherry pie. That will hold me over until school is out."

Ashleigh waved to their friends Jamie and Lynne as they looked for a place to sit. Their friends' table was already full, so she picked the one closest to her horse pals and introduced Emily.

Several minutes later, when Justin walked through the cafeteria doors, Emily waved him over to their table.

Justin smiled as he seated himself across from Ashleigh. "Thanks for the invite. I was afraid I was going to have to eat by myself," he said with a chuckle. "That's the worst part about going to a new school. It's pretty lonely until you make friends."

Ashleigh just smiled, feeling kind of awkward. She didn't have very many friends who were boys. She let the others do most of the talking while she finished her lunch. She was taking the last bite of her cherry pie and listening to Justin talk about his family's horses when Emily spoke up.

"I know!" Emily said enthusiastically. "Why don't we have Justin come to Edgardale after school today so he can see all of our horses?"

Justin smiled as he stood to leave, putting his plate

and empty milk carton back onto his tray. "That would be great! I've been hearing a lot about Edgardale's horses from some of the other kids in school," Justin said. "I'm anxious to see them. What would be a good time for you, Ashleigh?"

Ashleigh just about choked on her pie crust. What did Emily think she was doing? She couldn't just invite someone over without asking her parents' permission first. Especially a boy! "Uh . . ." Ashleigh hesitated as she pushed the uneaten meatloaf around on her plate.

Emily folded her napkin and laid it on the table. "Why don't you come over right after school?" she suggested. "Ashleigh and I have to move the horses around. That would give you a chance to see them all."

Justin nodded. "I have a few chores to do when I get home. But I'll saddle my horse and ride over right after that." He gave them another smile and went to dump his tray before heading to his afternoon classes.

Ashleigh just stared at Emily. Her cousin looked rather pleased about extending the invitation. *Is that the way she did things at home?* Ashleigh wondered. Didn't Aunt Gayle require that Emily get permission before inviting friends over? And what about all that talk of moving horses? Would Emily become brave just because Justin was there? Or had her cousin forgotten that she was afraid of horses?

Ashleigh walked to the cleanup counter to deposit

her tray before heading to her next class. One thing was for sure—things weren't going to be boring with Emily around.

"He's here," Caroline said as she leaned her pitchfork against the barn wall and peeked out the door for a better view. A big grin spread across her face. "He looks kind of cute from here, Ash."

Ashleigh socked her older sister in the arm. "He's just a *boy*," she said, glancing down the aisle to see where Emily was. "Emily, Justin is here," Ashleigh called to the end stall, where Emily was cleaning, before going out to meet him. Luckily her parents had said it was okay for Justin to visit. They, too, were anxious to meet the new neighbors.

"Wait until you see his horse, Ash," Caroline said as she brushed her long blond hair from her face and shaded her eyes against the late afternoon sun. "I think you'll like him."

Ashleigh stepped from the old brown barn and gasped when she saw the gelding Justin rode into the stable area. "He looks just like Stardust!" she said in surprise.

Justin dismounted in one graceful motion. "Isn't Stardust your mare?" he asked.

Ashleigh ran her hand down the chestnut's long white blaze, which was so much like her own horse's marking. "What's his name?"

"Jocko," Justin said, handing Ashleigh the reins. "Would you like to ride him?"

Ashleigh bobbed her head eagerly. It had been so long since she had been able to ride Stardust, and she was dying to get on something besides her brother's pony. She took the reins and grabbed a handful of mane. "Jocko's a couple of inches taller than my mare," she said as she stretched to reach the stirrup and pull herself into the saddle.

Emily strode from the barn. She stopped and stared. "Hey, I thought you weren't supposed to be riding Stardust until after she foaled."

Everyone laughed, and Ashleigh nudged the gelding, asking him to walk closer to Emily. "This is Jocko," Ashleigh said. "He's Justin's horse."

"Wow," Emily said, reaching out to stroke the chestnut gelding's soft nose. "He could be Stardust's twin, except he's not as fat as Stardust is right now."

Justin stepped next to Emily. "Ashleigh's going to take him for a canter. You can go next if you want."

Emily's face lit up but then fell. She shook her head. "I'd better not," she said, taking several steps away from the horse. "We've got a lot of chores to get done today."

Ashleigh smiled in sympathy at Emily's plight. Maybe if Jocko was a good mount, Justin would help them in their attempt to get Emily back on a horse. She lifted the reins, swinging the gelding toward the front paddock, and asked him for a trot. Jocko's stride was long and sweeping, just like a Thoroughbred's. "Is he a purebred?" she called back over her shoulder.

Emily, Caroline, and Justin lined the fence to watch Ashleigh ride. "He's only half Thoroughbred," Justin answered. "We're not sure what the other half is, but my parents think it might be Morgan."

"Stardust is half Thoroughbred, too," Emily said. "No wonder they look so much alike!"

Ashleigh trotted the gelding for another circuit and then asked him for a canter. Jocko responded immediately, switching to the correct lead as he floated across the ground. Ashleigh moved with the horse's motion, smiling as they sailed around the paddock in a perfect three-beat gait.

After a few more rounds she pulled the gelding to a walk and dismounted by the gate, handing the reins to Justin. "That was awesome!" she said as she patted the gelding's long, elegant neck. "I really missed doing that with Stardust. Riding Jocko made me feel like I was riding my own mare again."

"How much longer before she foals?" Justin asked, tying his gelding to the hitching post beside the barn.

"Stardust is due in just a few weeks," Ashleigh replied, thinking that Justin was pretty easy to talk to. He was certainly a lot better than that stupid bully who liked to pull her hair. She decided that she was going to like having Justin as a neighbor. "Come on, I'll show you my mare."

Ashleigh stopped to introduce Justin to her parents and Jonas. Justin invited them all down to see his family's farm on their next free day. "You should see his horse," Ashleigh told her parents. "Jocko looks just like Stardust!"

Mr. and Mrs. Griffen went to look at the gelding while Emily and Ashleigh led Justin to Stardust's stall.

Caroline grabbed a halter from the barn wall. "I'm going to start moving the broodmares back to their stalls," she said. "When you're finished, Ash, I could use some help."

Ashleigh nodded. Stardust also needed to go out for her turn in the paddock while her stall was being cleaned.

Justin was just as amazed by Stardust as Ashleigh had been by Jocko.

"I can't believe how much they look alike!" Justin said as he stood at Stardust's side, measuring her height against his body. "But you're right. Jocko is a few inches taller than your mare." He rubbed his hand across Stardust's swollen belly. "You're really lucky to own a mare," he said. "It would be so cool to have a foal from your very own mare!"

Emily handed Stardust's halter to Ashleigh. "My cousin takes really good care of Stardust," she said. "You should see how much she babies her." Emily got a far-off look in her eyes as she rubbed Stardust's fore-head. "I wish I had a horse of my own," she said for-lornly.

Justin helped Ashleigh buckle the halter. "I don't blame Ashleigh," he said with a grin. "I'm hoping my parents will give me my own foal to raise one of these days." He scratched Stardust's withers. "I get to help raise all of our foals, but I bet it's different when you know that the foal will be yours to keep."

Ashleigh nodded in agreement. Justin was a pretty neat kid. He seemed to understand exactly how she felt. She started to lead Stardust from the stall but then stopped, handing the rope to Emily. "I've got to help Caroline move the broodmares. Would you like to take Stardust out to the first paddock?"

Emily hesitated but finally took the rope from Ashleigh. Stardust was gentle, and Ashleigh knew she wouldn't give Emily any problems. It would be a good opportunity for her to gain some confidence and show Justin that she could handle the horses, too.

Ashleigh watched her walk the mare from the barn. When she was satisfied that Emily was doing okay, she went to gather the halters for the broodmares. A few minutes later, when she and Justin walked from the barn with their arms loaded with halters, Ashleigh was alarmed to see that Stardust was not in the front paddock, where Emily was supposed to put her. She quickly scanned the barnyard to see where Emily had taken her horse.

"There they are," Justin said, pointing to the far paddock.

"Oh, no!" Ashleigh cried as she dropped the halters and ran to where Emily stood tugging on Stardust's lead rope, trying to pull the mare away from the yearling colts she was touching noses with. They were the same colts her father had moved away from the other horses because they were coming down with an illness. Stardust had just been exposed to something that could harm her and her unborn foal!

6

"What are you doing?" Ashleigh cried, running up to her cousin.

Emily tugged at Stardust's lead rope, but the mare wouldn't move. Stardust made several small squeals and snorted as she conversed in horse talk with the two yearling colts. "She . . . won't . . . budge!" Emily grunted out as she pulled with all of her might, trying to get Stardust away from the sick colts.

Ashleigh grabbed the rope from Emily and used the end of it to pop her mare on the hindquarters to get her attention. Stardust swung her head in Ashleigh's direction, and Ashleigh used the opportunity to pull the pregnant mare away from the colts. When they were at a safe distance, Ashleigh turned to her cousin and frowned. "What happened, Em? You were supposed to put Stardust in the first paddock. How did you get all the way down here?"

Emily hung her head and began to cry. "I was going to put her where you told me, but Stardust was being so good, I thought that I'd take her for a longer walk." She shot the colts a disparaging glance. "I didn't know they would call her over to the fence." She wiped at her tears, trying to hide them from Justin. "Stardust dragged me over here. I couldn't stop her from going."

Ashleigh bit her lip to keep from saying anything more. She wanted to holler at Emily for the danger she had put Stardust in, but the truth was, it was as much her own fault for letting Emily go off on her own when she knew her cousin wasn't good with horses.

Justin scuffed the dirt with the toe of his riding boot. He looked from Emily to Ashleigh as if he was unsure of what to do. "Maybe it'll be all right," he said encouragingly. "She wasn't there for very long. Maybe Stardust didn't pick up any germs from the colts."

"I'm really sorry, Ash," Emily said. "I didn't do it on purpose. It's just that Stardust was behaving so well, I wanted to get more practice. That's why I walked her down here."

Ashleigh continued in silence. She didn't want to speak to Emily right then, but her cousin wouldn't go away.

"Just give me another chance, Ash," Emily begged. "I'll do exactly as you say from now on. It won't happen again."

Ashleigh sighed. The truth was, it didn't matter if it never happened again. Stardust had already been exposed. She'd have to tell her parents immediately. She'd overheard Jonas telling her father that he thought the colts might be coming down with the strangles. Strangles was a terrible illness in horses that caused a high fever, lack of appetite, and small swellings under their chins that broke open and leaked pus. It could also cause a pregnant mare to abort her unborn foal, or make her unable to nurse her foal if she was lucky enough to deliver it.

Justin nudged Ashleigh's arm to get her attention. "I think I'd better go home. It's getting late," he said as he shifted from foot to foot. "I'll see you two in school tomorrow."

Ashleigh nodded, then turned and walked Stardust to the paddock. Emily followed along behind, jogging to catch up with Ashleigh's long, angry strides.

"I'm really sorry, Ash," Emily said as she closed the gate behind Stardust. "Will you at least speak to me?"

Ashleigh hung the lead rope on the fence. She gave Emily a doubtful look. "I've got to go tell my parents about this. I don't really want to talk about it right now."

Then she turned on her boot heels and stomped away, leaving Emily to stare after her.

•   •   •

Ashleigh moped around the house until dinnertime and then spent the rest of the evening in the barn with Stardust. Her mother found her in the mare's stall just before bedtime.

"Ashleigh," Mrs. Griffen said, poking her head into the stall, "what's done is done. There's nothing you can do. Why don't you come up to the house and get ready for bed?"

But Ashleigh stayed where she was, hunkered down in the corner of the stall with Stardust standing over her. She reached out to rub her mare's soft muzzle again, marveling at how silky it felt to the touch. She breathed in the warm horse scent and closed her eyes, wishing she could spend the night in the barn. "I don't want to see Emily," she admitted.

Elaine Griffen propped her elbows on the stall door and stared through the meager barn light to the corner that Ashleigh occupied. "Don't you think you're being a little hard on Emily?" she said. "She's going through a rough time right now, and it was an accident. You know Emily didn't expose Stardust to those horses on purpose."

Ashleigh crossed her arms, staring hard at the wall in front of her. "But if she had done what I asked, none of this would have happened," she said sullenly. "Emily was just trying to show off because Justin was there."

Mrs. Griffen smiled gently. "It sounds like there

might be a little bit of jealousy involved here," she observed.

Ashleigh frowned. Why would *she* be jealous of Emily? Emily was afraid of horses and couldn't even ride.

"Look, Ash," Mrs. Griffen continued as she opened the stall door and motioned for Ashleigh to come out, "I know Emily has been hogging time with Mona, and now she's trying to be friends with the new boy. But you've got to understand that she must be very lonely, and now she has the opportunity to make new friends. You told me that you were going to help her get over her fear of horses," she reminded Ashleigh. "Don't you think that's going to be a little difficult to do if you're not speaking to her?"

Ashleigh picked at a loose board on the barn wall, avoiding her mother's probing stare. She sighed. She knew her mother had a point. "Okay," she mumbled. "I'll make it up to Emily tonight."

Mrs. Griffen put her arm around Ashleigh's shoulders and guided her out of the barn. "The vet will be here tomorrow when you get home from school, Ash. I wouldn't worry too much about Stardust. All of our mares have had their shots."

But the next day when she got home from school, Ashleigh discovered that she did indeed have something to worry about.

Dr. Frankel was down with the two yearlings when

Ashleigh and Emily arrived for their afternoon chores. The weather had turned warmer, and the friendly vet with the graying dark hair had removed his jacket and was examining the colts in his short-sleeved shirt.

"How are they?" Ashleigh asked as she watched the vet run his hands under the chestnut colt's jaws, palpating the soft tissue between the two large bones.

Dr. Frankel frowned. "Not good," he said as he took out his thermometer to take the yearling's temperature. "Feel right here," he instructed, guiding her hands to the underside of the colt's jaw.

Ashleigh ran her hand across the soft skin. Her fingers detected three hard bumps, each about half the size of a golf ball. She turned her eyes quickly to the vet.

Dr. Frankel nodded. "Looks like strangles."

Ashleigh felt her stomach do a big flop. Why couldn't it be just a common cold? That wouldn't be half as dangerous as the strangles.

Mr. Griffen squeezed Ashleigh's shoulder. "Stardust should be okay, Ash. She received her strangles shot last spring. She should still be covered," he assured her. "Even if she should happen to come down with it, it would be a mild case."

Ashleigh jammed her hands deep into her pockets and tried to push back her tears. That information didn't make her feel any better. "But what about the foal?" she cried. "Isn't there something we can do? Can't we start her on antibiotics?"

Dr. Frankel finished with his examination and turned his attention to Ashleigh. "The problem with this illness is that antibiotics could drive the infection deep inside. See these bumps?" he said, referring to the lumps under the chestnut's chin. "In a few more days, when they become soft, we'll lance them and drain all the bad stuff out. The colts will start to improve after that."

Ashleigh furrowed her brow in confusion. "But why can't you give them the antibiotics to help them heal faster?"

Dr. Frankel packed his things back into his bag. "If I were to give these colts antibiotics now, those bumps might drain on the inside, and you'd have one very sick colt that might die," he said gravely. "It's best to just keep them someplace out of the elements and let the illness run its course."

He walked several paddocks over to where Stardust waited. "This mare has already been exposed, Ashleigh. If we start her on antibiotics, it might help—or it might do just the opposite. We're taking the chance of driving that illness deep, and that could cause serious problems with a pregnant mare, especially one so close to foaling." Dr. Frankel ruffled Ashleigh's dark hair. "It's your call, kiddo."

Ashleigh felt like a deflating balloon. All of her hope was abandoning her. Which decision was the right one? Giving her mare the medicine seemed like the logical thing to do, but what if she made the wrong choice and Stardust got sick enough to lose her foal? She rubbed her stomach, hating the queasy sensation that overcame her. She felt cold inside. She looked to her mother and father. "What should I do?"

Mr. Griffen nodded toward the vet. "I think I'd ask the doctor here what he thinks would be best."

Ashleigh turned to the doctor expectantly. This was too big a decision, and she didn't have enough knowledge to make it on her own. "What would you do if Stardust were your horse?" she asked.

Dr. Frankel rubbed the back of his neck as he studied the chestnut mare. "I'm not fond of pumping pregnant mares full of drugs that they might not need," he said. "It is possible that she won't get the illness. If it were my horse, I'd wait and see what happens."

Ashleigh closed her eyes and hugged Stardust's neck, feeling the mare's warmth sink into cold skin. She hoped she was doing the right thing. But the vet was right. There wasn't anything they could do besides wait and see. She opened her eyes and saw Emily staring at her. Her cousin's eyes were bright with tears, and she looked as miserable as Ashleigh felt.

She knew she should be mad at Emily for being the

66

cause of all of this, but oddly enough, at that moment she felt sorry for her. She gave Emily a brave smile. "It'll be okay, Em," Ashleigh said. "You can help me take care of Stardust the next few weeks. We'll make sure that she doesn't get sick."

Emily returned her smile and handed Ashleigh Stardust's halter. "I'd like that," she said. "And from now on I'm going to do exactly what you say, Ash. I want to be good with horses, just like you are."

Mr. Griffen picked up the handful of halters that he had brought with him. "We don't have enough room in the barn for all of these yearlings," he said. "The weather's warm enough now that I think we can leave them out in the big pasture with the shelter. We'll keep the two sick ones quarantined where they're at."

Dr. Frankel nodded. "We're done with all the broodmares and the two sick colts. Let's get started with the shots for the new yearlings."

Ashleigh led Stardust from the paddock and handed the lead rope to Emily. "We'll be out to help in just a minute," she told her parents. "I want to get Stardust settled into her stall early tonight."

She walked beside Emily, watching how she handled the mare. She could tell that her cousin was a little nervous by the way she choked up on the lead rope. Stardust tossed her head, protesting the tight hold.

"Give her a little more rope," Ashleigh said. "You

67

only need to hold on that tight if a horse is giving you problems. Just relax and let her walk beside you."

Emily did as she was told, and Stardust settled down and walked quietly toward the barn.

Ashleigh watched as Emily reached out and gave Stardust a rub on the neck. Stardust gave Emily an affectionate nudge, and Ashleigh felt a twinge of jealously. Emily was already butting in on all of Ashleigh's friendships. She hoped her cousin wasn't trying to take over her horse, too.

They got Stardust bedded down in her stall and gave her an extra ration of grain, then went to help with the yearlings.

Dr. Frankel was just giving a shot to a small bay filly when Ashleigh and Emily arrived. The filly panicked when the needle was inserted into her neck, and she jerked away. They tightened a twitch on the end of the filly's nose to make her stand still, and finished with the shot.

"It looks like you guys have a lot of work to do with these horses," Dr. Frankel observed as he scratched the filly's thick coat.

Mr. Griffen nodded. "We'll worm them all tomorrow and then start working with them the following day," he said. "They need to be completely halter-broke and able to load into a trailer." He smiled at Ashleigh and Emily. "The girls are anxious to get their hands on these yearlings and get to work," he said.

Mrs. Griffen handed Ashleigh a halter. "That gray filly is pretty friendly, Ash. Could you catch her and bring her over to the doctor?"

Ashleigh climbed the fence and went to fetch the young horse with the black mane and tail. The filly eyed her warily as she approached. "Here, girl," Ashleigh said as she stepped softly and extended her hand, exposing a carrot that she had shoved into her pocket and forgotten to feed to Stardust.

The filly's ears pricked and she flared her nostrils, smelling the crunchy treat that Ashleigh held in her hand. "Come on, girl. It's all yours," Ashleigh crooned as she stopped in front of the yearling and waited for her to take the treat.

The gray extended her neck and stretched her lips to take the carrot. As she munched happily, Ashleigh gently touched the filly's cheek and moved back toward her neck. When the gray stood patiently, Ashleigh slipped the halter quietly over the filly's dainty muzzle and buckled it over her head. "That's a good girl," she said triumphantly as she walked the gray over to the vet.

"Here, I'll take her," Mr. Griffen said, reaching for the lead rope.

Ashleigh handed the lead to her father and stepped

to the side, waiting for the vet to administer the shot.

The gray filly cocked her ears as the vet came near, following his movement by rolling her eyes until the whites showed. Ashleigh saw the filly's muscles tense as the needle poked into her neck.

With a frightened snort, the gray filly jerked away from the veterinarian, tossing her head and catching Mr. Griffen in the side of the face. Ashleigh sucked in her breath as she watched her father stumble backward, the lead rope wrapping around his forearm as he flailed his arms for balance.

In the next instant the frightened filly pulled against the pressure of the rope, jerking Derek Griffen off his feet.

"No!" Ashleigh cried. She looked on in horror as the terrified yearling began backing up at a rapid pace, dragging her father across the field.

7

"Dad!" Ashleigh cried as she ran forward to help her father.

Mrs. Griffen was right behind her. "Ashleigh, be careful!" she shouted.

The gray filly pricked her ears at their yelling and backed up even faster, keeping the rope so taut that Mr. Griffen couldn't get his arm untangled.

Ashleigh slowed her steps, waving her arm to signal her mother to stop. "Easy, easy," she crooned in a soft voice as she inched toward the frightened filly. "Whoa, girl."

The gray filly slowed her pace, flicking her ears in Ashleigh's direction but keeping her frightened eyes on the person she was dragging. The more Ashleigh talked, the slower the filly moved, until she came to a stop, blowing suspiciously toward the downed man as her nostrils flared to take in his scent.

Ashleigh moved quietly, knowing that any sudden noise or movement could set the filly off again.

"I'm okay, Ash," Mr. Griffen said through gritted teeth as he quickly unwound the rope from his forearm.

Ashleigh stepped softly toward the filly with her hand outstretched, watching as the gray's untrusting eyes studied her movements, trying to determine if she should stay or flee.

"That's a good girl," she murmured. "Easy does it." She reached out and grabbed the lead rope, which was now hanging loose since her father had freed himself. "Gotcha," she whispered as her hand tightened around the lead. She stepped to the filly's side and rubbed her neck, speaking softly to her. When the gray heaved a sigh and worked her mouth, Ashleigh knew that she had the filly's trust.

Ashleigh's mother reached her father and checked him for injury, then hugged him tightly. "Don't scare us like that, Derek," she said sternly, and then hugged him again. "You could have been badly hurt."

Mr. Griffen took the filly from Ashleigh, taking a moment to give the gray a reassuring rub before leading her back to the vet. "When you work with horses, especially young ones, there's always a chance for an accident," he said as he rolled his shoulder and winced. "But, thanks to Ashleigh, I'm fine." He gave his daughter a grateful nod.

"I think we should put the rest of these yearlings in the stocks for their shots," Mrs. Griffen said. "There's no sense taking any more chances. The remaining yearlings are all colts, and they're a lot bigger than this little gray."

When Ashleigh got back to the fence, Emily was grinning from ear to ear.

"You were awesome, Ash!" Emily gushed. "I can't believe you just jumped in there and stopped that filly from dragging your dad. I wish I were as brave as you."

Dr. Frankel gave Ashleigh a thumbs-up. "You were pretty spectacular out there, kiddo," he said with a grin. "Your father could have been really hurt."

Ashleigh just looked at the ground, feeling the heat rise to her cheeks. "I just did what I had to do," she told everyone. "I didn't want to see my dad get hurt."

Emily looked at Ashleigh with admiration in her eyes. "Don't be embarrassed, Ash. You were great! I can't wait to tell my mom tonight when she calls. And tomorrow everyone at school will be excited to hear about it!"

Ashleigh's head snapped up. "Emily, it was nothing, really. Please don't go telling everyone at school."

"But you're a hero, Ashleigh! I'm really proud. The kids at school would be, too," Emily said.

Ashleigh sighed. She wasn't a hero, and she hoped she could talk Emily into keeping her mouth closed at school the next day. It was bad enough that Emily tried to copy everything she did. Now her cousin was building her up to be something she wasn't. Ashleigh scooped up the extra halters and frowned. She was just plain Ashleigh, and she liked it that way!

The following morning Ashleigh got up a half hour early so she could finish her chores and get to the bus stop before Emily. She missed her private conversations with Mona, and she had some things she wanted to discuss with her friend before Emily got there.

She arrived at the barn just as Jonas was mixing the morning grain.

"Good morning, Ashleigh," the old stable hand said as he pointed to the bucket that was Stardust's. "Where's your sidekick this morning?"

Ashleigh pressed her lips together to stop the mean remark she was about to make. "She's still in bed. I got up early so I could spend some time by myself."

Jonas poured wheat germ oil over the grain and smiled knowingly. "Sometimes we're put in situations that we wouldn't have chosen to be in," he said. "But these things have a way of working themselves out over time. Have patience, Ashleigh. Just like you do with those young horses," he advised.

Ashleigh picked up Stardust's ration of grain, pausing to think about what Jonas had just said. She knew she should have more patience with her cousin, but it was hard to do when Emily was quickly becoming a huge pest! She smiled her thanks at Jonas and went to feed and groom her mare and do her morning chores. She went over Stardust from head to hoof. So far her mare didn't seem to be showing any signs of the illness. Ashleigh crossed her fingers.

"You're *not* going to come down with the strangles, you hear?" she said as she watched the mare bolt down her morning grain. Ashleigh smiled. From the looks of her mare's appetite, she was sure Stardust was fine. She finished brushing the mare and picking her stall, then waved to Jonas as she headed out of the barn. She was just stepping through the doorway when Emily arrived.

"You're finished already?" Emily asked in surprise.

Ashleigh nodded. "I'll see you in a little while." She turned and hurried out the door before Emily could ask a bunch of questions. When she got to her room, she quickly dressed for school, pulling on a red shirt and a pair of blue cotton pants. She pulled her hair back into a ponytail and went to brush her teeth.

When she was done, she raced down the stairs, grabbing her schoolbooks from the desk and cramming them into her bag. She tossed in the latest horse magazine just in case she had some extra time to peek at it.

From the downstairs living room, Ashleigh called Mona and asked her friend to show up at the bus stop a few minutes early so they could talk in private.

Ashleigh skipped the breakfast of oatmeal and toast her mother had prepared, instead grabbing a banana and muffin from the counter. "I've got to meet Mona at the bus stop early today," Ashleigh explained.

Mrs. Griffen grabbed a small carton of orange juice from the refrigerator and handed it to Ashleigh. "What about Emily?" she asked. "Shouldn't you wait for your cousin?"

Ashleigh shifted the book bag high onto her shoulder and put her hand on the doorknob, preparing to leave. "I just wanted to spend a little time alone with Mona," she admitted. "The bus stop is only at the end of our driveway. Emily can walk that by herself, or she can wait for Caroline."

"All right, Ash," Mrs. Griffen said. "But let's not make a habit of it. Emily enjoys your company. We're going to start on the yearlings tonight, and I expect you to help your cousin learn her way around the young horses."

Ashleigh stuffed a big bite of muffin in her mouth and nodded as she walked out the door. Emily was coming up the path to the house, and Ashleigh could see the puzzled look on her cousin's face.

"You're going to school without me?" she said with a fallen face.

Ashleigh took a swig of the orange juice. "I have some things I need to talk to Mona about, so I thought I'd go to the bus stop a little early," she explained. "I'll see you there when you're done with breakfast." She turned and headed down the driveway, leaving Emily staring after her.

Mona was already waiting at the bus stop when Ashleigh got there.

"What's up?" Mona asked as she laid her books on the bench her father had built for them to sit on while they waited for the bus each morning.

Ashleigh set her books beside Mona's and sat down to rest. "It's Emily," she said, peeling her banana and taking a bite. She chewed slowly while she thought about what she wanted to say. She swallowed, and the fruit didn't go down very well. "My cousin is driving me crazy!" she finally admitted.

Mona plopped down next to Ashleigh and pulled a granola bar out of her pocket. "Emily seems pretty nice to me," she said. "Maybe it's just because you're not used to having her around. What's she doing that bothers you?"

"Everything!" Ashleigh cried. "She hogs all my time with you, and when Justin was here, she was with him every second. She invites people over without asking, and she always tries to wear the same clothes I do! And to make matters worse," she pouted, "Emily's trying to buddy up with Stardust."

Mona nodded in sympathy, then turned to look over her shoulder. "Don't look now, Ash, but your twin sister is coming down the driveway," Mona teased.

Ashleigh's head snapped around and her mouth turned down in a grim line. Emily was jogging down the driveway with her backpack bumping up and down on her back. She had on a red pullover shirt and a pair of blue pants. Ashleigh could see that her cousin's long dark hair was pulled back in a ponytail. She quickly pulled her hair band out of her hair and finger-combed it so it hung straight down her back. "See what I mean?" she complained.

Mona tried to hide a smirk, but she ended up sputtering laughter when she saw the agonized look on Ashleigh's face. "I'm sorry, Ash, but you should see your face right now. You look like you've been sucking on a lemon." She patted Ashleigh's shoulder. "Don't worry. I'm sure it's just a phase she's going through. Emily's trying to fit in, and she wants to be like you."

Emily huffed and puffed, setting her books down while she gasped for air. "My mom called right before I left the house. I came as quickly as I could. Did I miss anything?" she said between big gulps of air.

Ashleigh shook her head. "I was just getting ready to

tell Mona about how we're going to start working with your yearlings tonight."

"Great!" Emily said as she wiggled in between Ashleigh and Mona. "Let's start making our plans right now. We can finish them at lunchtime if we don't get them done by the time the bus gets here."

Ashleigh repeated what her mother had told her the night before. Once she began talking about the horses, Emily showed such an interest that it wasn't so bad being around her. She just wished she could ignore the fact that Emily was wearing practically the same clothing. She hoped the kids at school didn't notice.

The bus roared over the hill, and everyone stood and gathered their things. Ashleigh gave up all hope of sitting with Mona when Emily crowded right next to her friend and got on the bus ahead of Ashleigh. At least Ashleigh got a seat to herself this time, with no one pulling her hair.

Ashleigh spent the drive to school looking out the window at the greening countryside. Here and there broodmares grazed on the short new Kentucky bluegrass as their long-legged foals nursed or played at their side.

Ashleigh smiled dreamily. It wouldn't be long before Stardust would foal. What would the baby look like? Would it be dark like its father, or chestnut like her mare? There was now a registry that would take half Thoroughbreds as performance horses. With Renegade's Jockey Club papers, she'd be able to register this new foal as a performance horse!

They pulled into the schoolyard, and when the girls got off the bus, Ashleigh followed Mona and Emily into the school. Daydreaming about Stardust's foal had made her feel much better. She even managed a big smile for Emily.

But the smile quickly faded when she got to her first-period class. Before Mrs. Wilson could get the lesson started, Emily waved her hand wildly. When the teacher acknowledged her, Emily told her that she had something to share with the class.

Ashleigh cringed and her face flamed bright red as Emily began the story of how Ashleigh had saved her father. Ashleigh ducked her head as everyone in the class turned her way and applauded. She sighed in resignation. Jonas had told her she needed to have patience with Emily. But Ashleigh didn't think there was enough patience in the world to put up with her cousin.

8

At lunchtime Emily did it again. Even though Ashleigh had warned her that she wasn't supposed to invite any-one over without first asking permission, Emily got carried away during their lunch conversation with Justin and invited him to come help with the yearlings after school.

Truthfully, Ashleigh was glad that Justin had accepted. She had to admit she enjoyed his company. But now she had to go home and tell her parents that Emily had slipped up again.

When they got home from school, Ashleigh found a note on the kitchen counter telling her that her mother and father were out gathering the yearlings and would meet them at the horses' paddock.

"Come on, Em," Ashleigh said as she trotted up the stairs to their bedroom to change out of her school clothes. "Make sure you wear your boots. Sometimes the yearlings get a little rambunctious, and you might get your toes stepped on."

Emily froze on the bottom step. "I don't want to get hurt," she said in a small voice.

Ashleigh looked over the rail to where Emily stood, seemingly glued to the spot at the bottom of the staircase. She could see the fear on her cousin's face. She immediately felt guilty for unintentionally bringing Emily's fears back.

"I can't work with the yearlings," Emily said, the panic rising in her voice. "I'm not good enough. I might get hurt. I want to stick with Stardust for a while."

Ashleigh sighed. "Look, Em," she said with enough patience to make Jonas proud, "I won't make you do anything that you can't handle. We'll just be brushing the horses and trimming their manes and tails," she assured Emily. "We won't be doing anything dangerous. We've got to build up your confidence. The only way that's going to happen is if you go out there and try."

Emily stood perched on the first step for several moments, and Ashleigh was afraid that she was going to flee, but after a minute her cousin put one foot in front of the other and made it up to the bedroom.

Ashleigh pulled a blue T-shirt from the drawer. She

saw Emily eye her choice of clothes. "Don't even think about wearing a blue shirt," Ashleigh warned.

Emily pouted. "I'm sorry, Ash. I just really like dressing like you," she said. "I want to be really good with horses, just like you are."

Ashleigh walked to Emily's dresser and rummaged around, finally choosing a green T-shirt. "Dressing like me won't help you, Emily. You've got to get out and work with the horses to ease your fears. That's the only thing that's going to help."

Emily took a deep breath and pressed her lips in a firm line. "I know, but it's just so hard," she admitted. "I keep remembering how much everything hurt after I fell."

Ashleigh nodded. "I know. I've fallen off a bunch of times myself."

Emily stared at her with wide eyes. "You have?"

Ashleigh reached for her jeans. "Of course I have," she said with a smile. "Haven't you ever heard that old saying, 'Never a cowboy who hasn't been thrown'?"

Emily looked puzzled. "What's that supposed to mean? I thought cowboys were supposed to be so good, they didn't get tossed."

Ashleigh laughed. "Of course they get thrown. Not real often if they're good, of course. But I think that saying means that cowboys ride so many horses, eventually there's always one that gets them. If you haven't been bucked off, then you haven't ridden very many horses."

Emily pulled on her jeans and shirt and frowned. "But I don't like that part of riding," she said.

Ashleigh grabbed her boots from the corner and tugged them on. "Nobody likes that part, Em. But you've got to make yourself get back in the saddle after you've been tossed. Otherwise, if you wait too long and you start thinking about it, you're too afraid to ride again."

Emily sighed and shook her head. "But I *am* scared, Ash. How do I fix that?"

Ashleigh led the way out of the bedroom and down the stairs. "The thing is, you've got to decide if your dream to ride and work with horses again is bigger than your fear of falling off," she said as she shouldered her way out the back door.

"Everyone falls off," Ashleigh continued. "Just because you fall off doesn't mean you always get hurt badly, the way you did. Accidents are a part of owning a horse," she said as they walked toward the big brown barn. "My dad is one of the best horsemen I know, but look at the trouble he got into yesterday. Sometimes things just happen with horses no matter how careful you are."

They reached the barn, and Emily hesitated.

Ashleigh smiled encouragingly. "It's your choice,

Em. Either you fight your fear and learn how to work with horses again, or you give up and watch from the fence line."

They heard a sharp neigh from the yearlings' paddock and looked up to see Midnight Flyer circling the paddock with his head held high and his mane and tail floating on the breeze.

"Look at him go!" Ashleigh said in awe. "That's the Thoroughbred breed at its best!"

Emily's eyes took on a faraway look, and she set her jaw. "I'm going to do it," she said, turning to Ashleigh with determination in her eyes. "I'm going to get back to riding again!" She let out the breath she was holding and gnawed at her bottom lip. "Just help me stick to it, okay, Ash? Don't let me go back on my word."

Ashleigh extended her hand to shake on it. "Don't worry, Emily. You'll be riding before you go back home," she promised.

They entered the barn, and Ashleigh grabbed Stardust's halter and lead rope. "I'm going to go get my mare. We'll start with her and work up to the yearlings." She left the barn and returned a few minutes later with Stardust walking slowly beside her.

Emily eyed the pregnant mare. "Boy, Ash, she's so big now, she almost waddles."

Ashleigh snapped Stardust into the crossties and ran her hand over the chestnut's heavy belly. "I hope she doesn't get much bigger," she said. "She looks like she's ready to pop right now."

Ashleigh got out the brush bucket and handed it to Emily. "Start with the rubber currycomb at her neck and work your way back to her tail, then come back to the front on the other side and do the same thing."

Emily pulled the oval black rubber currycomb out of the bucket and took a deep breath.

"You can do it, Em," Ashleigh said encouragingly. "All you're doing is brushing the horse. The worst that can happen is that you get your toe stepped on." She laughed.

Emily laughed, too. "Thanks, Ash. You forgot to mention getting bitten, and flipped in the face with her tail."

Ashleigh went to tell her parents that they would be out to help shortly. She just wanted to have a leading session with Emily and Stardust before they started on the yearlings.

"We'll see you in a few minutes," Mrs. Griffen said as she tied one of the yearlings to the fence.

When Ashleigh got back to the barn, she closed both of the doors. She saw Emily's puzzled look. "It's just a precaution," she said. "If we have another incident like the last time, I want to make sure Stardust can't get loose and take off."

Emily unsnapped the crossties and took hold of the

lead rope. Ashleigh could see her cousin's hands shaking from where she stood. "Just relax, Emily," she instructed. "It's just a fat ol' pregnant mare going for a walk down the barn aisle."

Emily took a deep breath and took her position at Stardust's left shoulder, just behind her head. "Let's go, girl," she said, clucking to make the mare step out.

"Good," Ashleigh said as she followed them down the barn aisle. "See, Emily? There's nothing to it."

Stardust spotted the bale of alfalfa at the end of the aisle and began to pull on the lead rope.

"She's doing it again!" Emily groaned as she hung on to the rope, allowing herself to be pulled along by the mare.

"Get after her!" Ashleigh hollered. "Don't let her intimidate you. You're the boss. Pull on the lead rope *now!*"

Emily pursed her lips and dug in with her heels, giving a solid jerk on the rope. Stardust hesitated and stretched her nose out one more time, trying to reach the hay.

"No!" Emily said firmly as she kept a death grip on the lead line. "You're not going to bully me this time!"

Stardust halted and came back to Emily's side, shoving her with her nose and lipping her shirt. Emily smiled proudly and giggled as the whiskered muzzle nuzzled her face.

"See?" Ashleigh said. "You can do it, Emily. You've

just got to remember that *you're* the boss. Now let's put Stardust back out in her paddock so Rory and Caroline can clean her stall. We'll bring her back inside when we're done with the yearlings."

Emily held her head high as they walked to the yearlings' paddock. "I can't wait to tell my parents about this," she said eagerly. "My mom was worried that I'd never handle horses again, but I think I'm going to be able to do it, Ash!"

Ashleigh smiled. She was glad her cousin was making progress. But as they drew closer to the yearlings, Emily seemed to hesitate. Ashleigh watched as her cousin's steps slowed and her head drooped. "What's the matter?" Ashleigh asked.

Emily stopped next to Flyer as he was being tied to the fence. She stuck her hand through the fence, wiggling her fingers under the black colt's chin. "It's different with the yearlings," she said in a shaky voice. "They're not as well trained as Stardust."

Ashleigh put a comforting hand on Emily's shoulder. "That just means you have to pay closer attention to what you're doing," Ashleigh advised. "You're right, young horses are flightier and harder to work with, but we're going to be doing the same thing with them that you were doing with Stardust. All you have to do is brush them, Em. My mom, my dad, and Jonas will walk them."

Emily stood there while Flyer blew softly against her hand. She squared her shoulders and turned to Ashleigh. "Okay, let's do it."

"Here's your brushes, girls," Mrs. Griffen said as she handed a brush box to each of them. "Ashleigh, why don't you get Emily started on the bay colt at the end? He seems to be the most easygoing of the bunch."

Ashleigh nodded. She got Emily set up and took the seal brown filly next to him. "It's not that much different from working with Stardust," she told her cousin. "Just pay close attention to the signals the colt sends you," she instructed. "Watch his ears and the way he moves his muscles. Horses always telegraph when they're going to do something."

Emily nodded solemnly and picked up the first brush, scrubbing it over the bay colt's shaggy coat. "Yuck!" she said as she spit out several loose horse hairs. "These yearlings are really starting to shed."

Ashleigh laughed, but Emily was right. With the warm weather and the good food, the yearlings were shedding terribly. With every stroke she took, hair flew through the air. They were going to need a good shower when they were through.

Ashleigh kept an eye on Emily while she worked on her own horse. Everything was going fine until her cousin tried to pick the bay's front feet. The colt lifted his front foot and then set it down quickly before

Emily could clean it. She tugged at the foot. "Now he won't lift it at all," she grunted.

"Here, let me show you a trick," Ashleigh said as she stooped by the colt's front leg. "Just put your fingers at the bottom of this long tendon and squeeze a little." She demonstrated the move, and the colt immediately picked up his foot, then set it right back down again. Ashleigh tried a few more times, but each time the colt lifted the foot for only a moment and then put his full weight on the leg, forcing it back to the ground.

Ashleigh gave the colt a warning swat at the girth and the colt flicked his tail to show his displeasure. The next time she tried the foot, he wouldn't budge at all. Ashleigh huffed. "Looks like we're going to have to try something a little more drastic with this guy," she said as she lifted the hoof pick that Emily had laid on the ground.

Emily craned her neck to see. "If you can't get his foot up, how are you going to use the hoof pick?"

Ashleigh grinned. "I'm going to use the pick to get his foot up." At her cousin's confused look, Ashleigh explained. "If the other way doesn't work, you take the end of the pick and apply a slight amount of steady pressure just above the hoof line." She pressed the colt lightly, and the bay lifted his foot and set it down again. Ashleigh poked him once more. She continued until the bay held his foot for her to clean. "See?" she said triumphantly. "The pressure doesn't hurt them, but it's enough to be a bother, so they lift the foot."

Emily reached for the hoof pick. "Let me try."

"Be careful with the back ones, Em," Ashleigh warned. "A horse can cow-kick you with their hind legs."

After the lesson with his front foot, the bay colt was more willing to hold up his other feet to be cleaned. Emily was on the last hoof when the yearling decided he'd had enough.

"Yikes!" Emily cried as the colt set his foot down on her boot. "Ouch!" Emily pushed on the gelding, trying to pull her foot out from under his hoof.

Ashleigh jumped to Emily's aid, pushing the colt at the shoulder to get him to move over. The yearling stepped over, eyeing the girls with a look of innocence.

"Are you okay?" Ashleigh cried as she looked at the hoof mark on her cousin's right foot.

Emily flexed her foot, wiggling the toes within the boot. "He only got the edge," she said in relief as she continued to work her foot.

Ashleigh scrunched up her lips. "Are you going to be all right, Em? Do you want to keep going?"

Emily grinned. "I suppose we should have another saying," she said with a laugh. "Never a horse girl that hasn't been stepped on!"

Ashleigh shared the laugh with Emily. "Attagirl, Em!

Don't let them scare you. You can do this."

They moved down the line to work on the next set of yearlings. When they came to the last ones, Justin rode up on Jocko. He waved to everyone and dismounted.

"Emily said you guys might like some help with your yearlings," he volunteered.

Ashleigh exchanged a quick look with her parents. She had forgotten to tell them about Emily's latest invitation.

Mrs. Griffen smiled and motioned Justin over. "You're always welcome here, Justin," she said. "We can certainly use an extra pair of hands."

Ashleigh breathed a sigh of relief. "What's next?" she asked.

Derek Griffen nodded toward the front pen. "We're going to teach everyone to lunge on a line," he said. "Most of these yearlings learned how to do this when they were about ten months old, but your aunt and uncle didn't keep up with it once Robert got sick."

They took the yearlings two at a time to the front paddock. Ashleigh ran to get the lunge lines while her father and Jonas picked opposite corners to work the young horses.

Ashleigh watched proudly as her father snapped the twenty-foot-long lunge line onto the yearling he held and taught the colt to move in a circle around him.

Once the colts were going well at a walk, trot, and canter, the adults turned them over to Ashleigh and Justin to work for a few minutes while they went to get the next set of yearlings. Mrs. Griffen and Caroline walked the horses cool after their exercise, and Emily and Rory brushed them down before they were put away.

Ashleigh was impressed with how much Justin seemed to know. He was very calm around the colts and didn't let them get away with any tricks. By the time the last horse was put away, everyone was hot and dirty, but they all had smiles on their faces. They had done a good day's work, and the yearlings had made great progress.

So had Emily.

Mrs. Griffen patted Emily on the back as they put away the lunge lines and brushes. "You did a great job today, Em!" she complimented the girl.

Emily beamed proudly. "I did, didn't I?" she said to Ashleigh.

Ashleigh nodded. "A couple more days like this and you might be ready to start riding," she said.

Emily shook her head. "I don't want to wait a couple of days. I want to start now," she protested. "And I want to start with Stardust!"

9

Ashleigh swallowed hard. Emily had already had an accident with every horse she'd touched at Edgardale. When she and Emily had first made plans, Ashleigh had hinted that she might let her cousin ride Stardust at a walk. The mare's pregnancy wouldn't allow for any more than that. But did she really want to take the chance that Emily might make a mistake and end up hurting herself and Stardust?

"Come on, Ash," Emily cajoled. "I know I can do this! Stardust is such a great mare. She'll be perfect for me to start with."

Justin stepped into the conversation. "You can ride Jocko if you want," he politely offered.

Emily eyed the chestnut gelding and shook her head. "I don't think he'd be a good horse for me to start with," she said. "I saw Ashleigh galloping him in the paddock the other day, and he looks like he can go pretty fast. Stardust is so big now, she won't do anything but walk."

Ashleigh looked to her parents, but they weren't any help at all.

Mrs. Griffen shrugged. "I don't see that it could hurt anything," she said.

Ashleigh felt like letting out a big, fat snort. *Of course it could hurt! Look at the problems Emily's had so far.*

Mr. Griffen handed Ashleigh Stardust's bridle. "I don't think you'll be able to get the saddle girth around her. Emily will have to ride bareback."

Emily's eyes widened. "Bareback?" she squeaked. "I can't ride bareback. I'll fall off!"

Ashleigh suppressed a smile, pretending to be disappointed that Emily wouldn't be able to ride Stardust. "I'm sorry, Emily, but my dad is right. Stardust's saddle won't fit her right now. If I ride her for light exercise, I always go bareback. She won't be able to use her saddle again until after she foals."

Emily shoved her hands into her pockets and scowled. She looked to where Stardust was grazing in one of the front paddocks. "Okay, I'll do it," she said finally. "You can put a lead rope on her and walk with me, right?"

Ashleigh grudgingly nodded and went to get Stardust. Emily was right about that. She would definitely have a lead rope attached. There was no way she was going to turn her horse loose with her cousin.

Wherever Stardust and Emily went, Ashleigh would be right there beside them, making sure everyone was safe.

Justin helped Ashleigh catch Stardust and bridle her, then gave Emily a leg up. "Don't be so nervous," he said. "I can feel you shaking right now. If your horse feels it, she'll get nervous, too. Take a deep breath and relax, Em."

Emily bit her bottom lip and lifted the reins. Her fists closed around the leather, holding on so tightly that her knuckles turned white.

Ashleigh pried Emily's fingers open. "Just hold them lightly, Em. You remember how. Close your fingers lightly around the reins and keep a little contact with Stardust's mouth," she instructed. "I'll be holding her, so she's not going to run off. Just hold on with your legs and keep your balance. Stardust will do the rest."

Ashleigh clucked for the mare to move forward at a walk. She heard the sharp intake of Emily's breath as Stardust stepped off. Emily panicked, squeezing her legs and jerking on the reins. Stardust shifted uneasily at the mixed signals and tossed her head.

Emily cried out in fright, "She's going to run off!"

"Calm down!" Ashleigh hissed. "I've got her. She can't run off with you."

Emily loosened the reins and took several faltering breaths. "I'm sorry, Ash. I just get so scared when I think something is going to happen."

Ashleigh stopped Stardust and turned to Emily. "Em, this isn't going to work if you don't get control of your fear," she scolded. "If you keep snatching the reins tight and clamping Stardust's rib cage every time you *think* something might happen, you're never going to be able to ride again. *You* are going to cause your horse to do something bad if you keep acting this way."

Emily bowed her head. "I know," she said. "I just can't help it."

Justin entered the paddock. "How about if I walk beside you and help steady you on Stardust?" he offered.

Emily nodded.

"Okay, here we go," Justin said. "Keep your concentration focused on your balance, Emily, just like you used to do when you rode all the time."

Ashleigh held her breath as she asked Stardust to move forward again. Out of the corner of her eye, she saw Emily begin to tense, but Justin kept his hand on her leg to steady her balance. After a few steps Emily seemed to grow more comfortable, and the tension went out of her hands. Stardust settled into a nice walk, and they made several rounds of the pen.

"I think that's good enough for one day," Justin said as he released Emily's leg. "I can come over and help some more this week if it's all right with your parents, Ashleigh."

Ashleigh smiled gratefully. It would probably take

the two of them to get Emily back to riding again.

Emily smiled triumphantly. "I want to call my mom and tell her all about this," she said proudly.

Justin grabbed his bridle off the fence and went to get Jocko out of the adjoining paddock. "I'll see you girls at school tomorrow."

Ashleigh waved goodbye to their new friend. "Come on, Em. We've got to get Stardust put away and then go check on those two sick colts. My mom says they've got pretty high temperatures. When we get that done, you can call home."

She led Stardust back to the barn and inspected her nostrils for any sign of a runny nose and the underside of the mare's chin for strangles bumps. She breathed a big sigh of relief when all seemed fine. Stardust was going to be okay.

The following week passed in a blur of activity. Every night after school, Ashleigh helped her parents work with the yearlings while Emily helped Caroline and Rory clean stalls. Justin came over every day to help coach Emily. She was making small improvements, but every time Stardust bobbled or sneezed, Emily still panicked.

Aunt Gayle came to visit on the weekend, and

everyone enjoyed her company. Emily stuck close to her mother's side, spending every extra minute she could in her company. Aunt Gayle was happy to report that Uncle Robert's condition had improved quite a bit and that he would be coming home from the hospital when she returned.

At the end of the following week, Ashleigh was taking the bridle off of Stardust when she noticed that the mare's ears seemed warmer than usual. Ashleigh went to the tack room medicine cabinet to get out the thermometer. When she returned, Stardust gave a series of short coughs.

"Easy, girl," Ashleigh said as patted the chestnut. "Let's have a look in your mouth and see if you've got something stuck in there." She put her hand under Stardust's chin and was attempting to lift her upper lip when she saw mucus in Stardust's left nostril. "Oh, no, you don't!" she said with resolve. "You're *not* going to get sick."

She quickly took the mare's temperature. When the digital thermometer beeped, she checked the numbers and felt her stomach roll. Stardust's temperature had already gone up to 102 degrees. A horse's normal body temperature was 101 degrees. It wasn't a big jump, but it could be the start of an uphill climb if her mare was sick.

Ashleigh's hands began to shake. She closed them in tight fists to stop the shaking. *This can't be happening!*

Slowly she reached out and felt along Stardust's jaw-bone, afraid of what she might find there. Her breath whooshed from her lungs as her fingers moved over three hard bumps that were just starting to form.

What was she going to do? This wasn't supposed to happen! Ashleigh ran to get her parents.

"We'd better separate her out from the rest of the broodmares," Mr. Griffen said. "We don't want this going through the whole barn."

Mrs. Griffen set aside the foaling charts she was studying. "We could put her out with the other two sick colts," she suggested.

Ashleigh shook her head adamantly. "No, I want her here in the barn."

"Ashleigh," Mrs. Griffen said, "we can't expose all the other mares and foals to this illness. You know how the strangles work. Stardust will have a horribly runny nose, and those bumps will break and spread the germs everywhere. We've got to keep her isolated."

Mr. Griffen put a comforting hand on Ashleigh's shoulder. "Look, Ash, I know this is your mare and you're very concerned about her, but we have to look after the welfare of the other horses, too. I think the best place to put Stardust would be Renegade's summer paddock. There's a nice shelter there, and it's separate from the other horses. Let's go move her over there now."

Ashleigh followed her parents to Stardust's stall. Her boots felt as though they were made of lead. It was an effort to lift them one at a time as she moved slowly down the barn aisle.

Why is this happening? Stardust having a foal was her dream come true. And now she could lose it all because of a stupid illness that Emily's horses had brought.

They reached the stall, and Ashleigh slipped the halter over Stardust's head. She knew it wasn't fair, but at the moment she was very angry at her cousin for coming to Edgardale and bringing the sick colts. Emily had been a pain ever since she arrived, and now Stardust was sick and could possibly lose her foal because of Emily's horses.

Emily materialized around the corner as they were leading Stardust to the stallion's summer paddock. "Where are you taking Stardust?" she asked as she fell into step beside Ashleigh.

Ashleigh pressed her lips together and kept walking, ignoring the shocked look on her parents' faces. She didn't want to speak to Emily right then. She didn't even want to look at her cousin. Ashleigh kept her eyes facing forward as she trudged toward the stallion's paddock. Her insides felt as though they were being twisted in knots.

"Ash?" Emily jogged several steps to keep up with Ashleigh. "What's the matter? Is Stardust all right?"

Ashleigh took a deep breath. Her face was hot, and she felt like a volcano ready to erupt. She didn't dare open her mouth to speak, for fear that she'd say something hateful to her cousin that would get her grounded for life.

Mrs. Griffen put her arm around Emily's shoulders and steered her off to the side. "Emily, honey, Ashleigh isn't feeling very cheerful right now," she explained. "Stardust has come down with the strangles. Let's let her be by herself for a while."

Emily glanced at Ashleigh with wide, sympathetic eyes, then nodded. "I'll finish my barn chores and then be up for dinner." She ran back to the barn.

Ashleigh got Stardust settled into the new pen. She bedded the shed extra deep with straw and hung a hay net of fresh timothy. "How're you feeling, girl?" she asked as she dumped some grain into the feeder.

Stardust lipped the grain and took a small bite, chewing it slowly. Ashleigh was glad to see that she still had an appetite, but she couldn't ignore the fact that the mare wasn't attacking the feed with her usual gusto. Her heart sank even lower when Stardust left the grain half finished.

Mr. Griffen poked his head into the shed. "We called Dr. Frankel and asked him to come over tomorrow," he said. "Dinner will be ready in ten minutes. Finish up here and we'll see you up at the house."

Ashleigh lowered her eyes and poked at the straw bedding with the toe of her boot. "I'm not hungry," she said. "I'm going to stay here with Stardust."

"Look, Ashleigh," Mr. Griffen said as he ran a hand frustratedly through his dark brown hair, "I know you're feeling bad about this, but not eating isn't going to help Stardust. If you get sick, how is that going to help your mare?"

Ashleigh thought about it for a few moments and nodded. "I'll be up in a minute." She checked everything in the stall to make sure it was perfect, then threw her arms around Stardust's neck and buried her face in her soft mane. "You've got to get better," she pleaded. "The vet said that you might not get as sick, since you've already had your strangles shot. Please don't get any sicker, Stardust. I don't want you to lose your foal!"

She gave the mare one last pat and went to the house to wash up for dinner. The only seat left at the table was next to Emily. Ashleigh eyed the chair, trying to decide how much trouble she would get into if she just turned around and went to her room. But then she frowned. It *wasn't* her room anymore; it was a room she shared with Emily.

Ashleigh plopped down in the chair beside her cousin, hoping that Emily wouldn't speak to her. But she knew that was an impossible wish. Emily immediately started asking all kinds of questions about Stardust.

Mrs. Griffen passed the plate of pork chops. "Your cousin is talking to you, Ashleigh. I know you're unhappy right now, but don't be rude."

Ashleigh speared the smallest pork chop on the plate. "Stardust is getting sick," she grumbled. "She has a runny nose and a fever that's climbing." She took a small helping of broccoli and some scalloped potatoes and forced herself to eat. If she had a mouth full of food, surely her parents wouldn't expect her to speak.

Emily continued to ask questions, and Ashleigh answered them as briefly as she could.

Rory handed his piece of chocolate cake to Ashleigh. "You can have my dessert if it makes you feel better, Ash."

Ashleigh felt the first real flicker of a smile cross her face since she'd discovered that Stardust was sick. Rory loved horses as much as she did. He understood how bad she was feeling. "Thanks, kiddo," she said as she passed his dessert back to him and added her own. "It makes me feel better just knowing you're willing to share. But I'm not very hungry right now. How about if you eat my piece of cake, too?"

Rory nodded happily and dug in, smearing almost as much cake on his face as he got in his mouth.

Ashleigh turned her attention to her parents. "I want to sleep in the stall with Stardust tonight." She paused, crossing her fingers that they would say yes. Stardust needed her now. She wouldn't be able to sleep a wink if she had to stay in the house.

Mr. and Mrs. Griffen exchanged glances. "I think that would be all right," Mr. Griffen said. "The weather is getting warmer, and it might help your mare sleep better in that new stall if you're there with her. The last thing she needs right now is some extra stress."

Ashleigh asked to be excused and pushed back from the table. She had to get her sleeping bag out of the hall closet and prepare some snacks for later.

Emily set her fork on the plate with a clatter. "I want to sleep in the barn, too."

Ashleigh swung around to face her cousin. "No, Emily, I'm going to do this by myself," she said.

"But I want to stay in the barn with you!" Emily demanded. "Why can't I come, too?"

Ashleigh looked to her parents, pleading with her eyes for them to make Emily stay in the house. Surely they could see that she didn't want to spend a lot of time with Emily that night.

Mrs. Griffen shifted uneasily in her chair. "Emily, I think Ashleigh is feeling really bad and would like to be by herself right now. I think you should sleep in your room tonight. You've got school tomorrow."

Emily frowned and pushed her plate away. "Ashleigh has school, too," she reasoned.

Mr. Griffen folded his napkin and pushed away from the table. "Ashleigh can be excused from school tomorrow so she can be here when Dr. Frankel comes. You can catch up with her after school, Emily."

Ashleigh shot her parents a grateful look and ran up the stairs to get her things. She grabbed her sleeping bag, a flashlight, and some horse magazines. She was back down the stairs and out of the house before Emily could catch up to her.

She went to the barn first to tell Jonas that she would be spending the night with Stardust and to pick up the folding cot from the tack room. She had forgotten to get her snacks, and she didn't want to return to the house and risk running into Emily, so she grabbed some extra carrots from the bag. Carrots were Stardust's favorite.

But when she got to the stallion paddock where Stardust was stabled, it was obvious that the mare was in no shape to eat the special treat. Stardust stood with her head hanging low and her breath rasping in and out of her lungs as her big belly lifted and fell with each labored breath.

Ashleigh didn't need Dr. Frankel to tell her that Stardust was in deep trouble!

10

"Stardust!" Ashleigh ran to her mare's side and dropped to her knees in the deep bedding, taking the small chestnut's muzzle in her hands. Ashleigh grimaced when she saw the thick mucus that ran from the mare's nostrils. Stardust wheezed and coughed, shifting uneasily from foot to foot.

"Ashleigh?" Jonas's deep voice cut through the night as he stepped into the stall. "Oh, no," he said as he observed Stardust. "I'll get the thermometer and we'll see how bad her temperature is."

Jonas disappeared into the darkness and returned a few minutes later with the thermometer and some rags to clean the mare's nose. He took her temperature, setting his jaw when he read the results. "She's at one-oh-three-point-five," he said with a shake of his head. "If it climbs any higher, I'm going to start worrying about that foal."

Ashleigh felt as though the air had been knocked from her. "What can I do, Jonas?" she asked, feeling more helpless than she'd ever felt. "The vet says we can't give her any antibiotics. Is there anything else we can try?" Her shoulders slumped and she felt the tears rising in her eyes.

"All we can do now is wait it out," he said gently. "We could give her a little bute to help with the discomfort, but I don't like giving that to pregnant mares. Especially one so close to foaling and already in trouble." Jonas scratched the stubble on his chin. "I'll run up to the house and let your parents know that Stardust has gotten worse," he offered. "If you want to do something to help your mare, go to the tack room and get a blanket for when she gets the chills, and a bucket of water and a sponge for when she's hot with the fever."

Ashleigh gave Stardust one last pat and ran to the barn, gathering the things that Jonas had suggested. She saw the drench gun their trainer, Mike Smith, used for washing out a runner's mouth before a race, and grabbed that, too. Stardust didn't seem interested in drinking water, but Ashleigh knew that the mare would need it to keep from becoming dehydrated. The drench gun might come in handy.

Her parents were at the stall by the time she returned. Mrs. Griffen ran her hand across Ashleigh's hair and kissed the top of her head. "I'm sorry, honey. We were really hoping that it wouldn't come to this." She handed Ashleigh a tissue to wipe her eyes. "Rory sent you some snacks." She held up a small plastic bag with a squished peanut butter and jelly sandwich in it, and an apple. "I'll get everyone to bed and come back out to check on you again in a little while."

"Thanks, Mom," Ashleigh said as she helped her father set up the cot just outside the stall and spread the sleeping bag over the top of it. Later, after her parents had gone to bed, she'd move it into the stall with Stardust.

She said good night to her mom and dad and went back to tending her sick horse. A short while later her mother returned for a final check.

"If you need anything during the night, use the barn phone and call us," Mrs. Griffen said.

Ashleigh nodded and continued running her hand down Stardust's neck. The rubbing motion seemed to soothe the suffering mare.

Several minutes after her mother left, Ashleigh heard the soft tread of footsteps and thought her mother had returned again. She glanced up and was shocked to see Emily standing in the doorway with her sleeping bag and pillow tucked under her arms. Emily had changed into the same color shirt that Ashleigh had worn to dinner and was still wearing. "What are *you* doing here?" Ashleigh said in an accusing tone.

"I'm going to spend the night with you and help you take care of Stardust," Emily said as she unfolded her sleeping bag, preparing to spread it out next to Ashleigh's.

"Oh, no, you don't!" Ashleigh hurried from the stall. "You're not staying out here with me. Didn't my parents already tell you that you had to stay inside tonight?"

Emily sulked. "Ashleigh, I really don't want to stay in the house," she protested, her bottom lip sticking out in a stubborn manner. "I feel awful about this. I want to stay with you and help Stardust get better."

Ashleigh's hands curled into fists at her sides. She could feel her nails biting into her palms. She pressed her lips together to stop the flow of hateful words, but it was useless. Her mouth opened, and she couldn't stop all of the mean things she wanted to say.

"Stardust is sick because of *you!*" Ashleigh cried. "It was *your* stupid horses that brought the strangles to Edgardale. And it was *you* who let her go touch noses with them. If you had done what I asked and taken her straight to her paddock that day, Stardust wouldn't be sick!" She paused for a moment and thought of one thing more. "And take off that stupid shirt! Stop dressing like me!" she hollered. "You're driving me *crazy!*"

Her temper finally spent, Ashleigh was able to see through her cloud of anger, and what she saw made her feel terrible. Emily stood in the center of the stall doorway, looking very small as she clutched her pillow to her chest. Tears were streaming down her face.

Emily hiccuped and pushed her tangled brown hair out of her eyes. "I . . . I didn't do it on purpose, Ashleigh. All I wanted was to be good with the horses like you." She sniffed loudly, dragging the sleeve of her shirt across her nose. "You're so lucky. Your parents are both healthy, and you can ride the horses as much as you want without feeling scared. You've got this great mare, and you're so brave with horses that you can do anything. My parents won't even let me have a horse of my own. I dress like you because I want to *be* like you!"

Emily turned and ran toward the house, dragging the unfolded sleeping bag along the ground.

Ashleigh ran after her cousin, surprised at how fast Emily scrambled across the grass. She worked her arms to gain more speed as she followed her cousin pell-mell across the barnyard toward the house. When she drew closer, Ashleigh accidentally stepped on the sleeping bag Emily was dragging, causing Emily to bobble and slow her pace just a fraction. Ashleigh reached out and grabbed her cousin's arm, dragging her to a halt at the edge of the yard.

"Emily, stop!" she hissed in a loud whisper, not wanting her parents to hear their argument.

Emily swung around quickly, throwing Ashleigh off

balance. Ashleigh was surprised at the anger she saw in her cousin's eyes.

"You're just plain *mean,* Ashleigh," Emily said in a voice that was still raspy from crying. "I didn't want to have to leave my home and my parents, but after making big plans with you, I thought I'd have a great time here at Edgardale." She sniffed several times and angrily wiped at her tears. "All I wanted to do was be like you and be great with horses so I could ride again and make my parents proud. But you don't want to help me, and you don't like sharing your horse or your friends. I wish I'd never had to come here!"

Emily turned her back on Ashleigh and stomped toward the house, her spine as stiff as a fence post as she faded into the darkness.

Ashleigh let out the shocked breath she had been holding at Emily's sudden outburst. "Em, wait!" she called. "I'm sorry. I didn't mean all those horrible things I said. Don't go." She stood peering into the darkness, the chirping of crickets and other insects filling the cool night air as she strained to hear the sound of Emily's footsteps hitting the porch.

After a long moment Emily stepped back into Ashleigh's view. Ashleigh searched for a sign that her cousin was willing to talk, but Emily's pinched face was unreadable.

Ashleigh sighed and sank to the ground. Her legs

felt like rubber, and all of her strength seemed to have left. Only a short while before, everything had been great; now it seemed as though everything was falling apart. "I'm really sorry, Emily," she said softly. She pulled several blades of grass from the lawn and began shredding them. "I was really mad about Stardust getting the strangles, and I still am. But I know it's not really your fault. I'm just so scared that she's going to lose this foal."

Emily knelt in the damp grass next to Ashleigh. "Do you really mean it about being sorry?" she asked. "You didn't mean all of that stuff you said to me?"

Ashleigh started to nod but stopped. "Well, everything except the part about dressing like me," she said. "It's really embarrassing, Em, especially at school."

Emily pulled her knees up and rested her chin on them. "I guess I understand how you feel," she admitted. "I know I've been a pest, but it's just that I don't have any sisters or brothers, and there aren't very many kids where I live. I get kind of lonely, and I thought that maybe at Edgardale I could really be a part of everything."

Ashleigh stood and pulled Emily to her feet. "But you *are* a part of it, Emily. You've made friends with Mona and Justin and some of the kids at school, and you've made progress with your riding." She paused, trying to figure out how to say the next part without hurting Emily's feelings again. "The thing is, you shouldn't try to be me, Em. You need to be yourself."

Emily crossed her arms. "But you're so great with the horses!" she cried. "I want to be like that again."

Ashleigh walked Emily to the porch steps. "You can be a good horsewoman again if you work at it," Ashleigh said encouragingly. "It's just going to take some time. You had a pretty bad fall and you're still scared. But I'll help you work it out." She handed Emily the sleeping bag she had dropped. "You've just got to work hard at being Emily Daniels, horsewoman extraordinaire."

Emily smiled and gave Ashleigh a quick hug. "Are you sure you don't want me to sleep in the barn with you?"

Ashleigh shook her head. "You've got to go to school tomorrow. Go get some sleep and see me before you leave for the bus in the morning. Maybe Stardust will be better by then."

Emily smiled and gave her cousin a quick hug. Then she grabbed her things and headed back into the house. Ashleigh made her way back to Stardust's stall. The little chestnut was lying down, making her swollen belly look much bigger. It reminded Ashleigh of just how much there was to lose if things didn't get better.

Stardust groaned, and Ashleigh went to her side, kneeling in the straw as she ran her hands over the mare's sweat-soaked coat. "You're so hot," she said. "I'm going to get some water to sponge you off."

Ashleigh dipped the bucket into the drinking trough, filling it with cool water. She carried it back inside the stall and immersed the sponge, wringing it out a little before dragging it down Stardust's already damp neck.

Stardust heaved a sigh, telling Ashleigh that the water felt good. Ashleigh was careful not to get the mare too wet. It wouldn't take much for the fever to turn to chills, and then the extra water would be a problem.

Ashleigh finished the sponge bath and then sat in the straw, drawing Stardust's head into her lap. She combed her fingers repeatedly through the mare's silky forelock, speaking soft, reassuring words.

Stardust slept for a while and so did Ashleigh. But Ashleigh woke later to the sound of her mare's raspy breathing. Her air passages were so congested that she was having trouble taking a normal breath.

Ashleigh got Stardust to her feet to see if it would make it easier for her to breathe. Stardust shook the straw from her coat and began to cough. Ashleigh winced at the raw, painful sound, but Stardust blew her nostrils clear and was able to breathe better.

Ashleigh emptied the bathwater and drew a fresh bucket for drinking, but Stardust refused to take even a sip.

"Come on, girl," she pleaded. "You've got to drink something." She laid the bucket down and retrieved the drench gun. She put the tip of the gun in the water and pulled on the plunger, filling the gun with sweet, cool water.

"Here you go, girl." Ashleigh inserted the end of the gun into Stardust's mouth and tipped her chin up. She slowly pushed the plunger, allowing the water to run down the back of the mare's parched mouth.

Stardust worked her jaw, swallowing the cool liquid.

Ashleigh refilled the gun several times before letting Stardust lie down again. This time she seemed to rest a little easier, but her fever was still high. Ashleigh continued with the sponge baths every hour to help keep Stardust's temperature down.

By morning, when her parents and Jonas checked in on her, Stardust didn't seem any better.

Mr. Griffen checked the thermometer. "Well, the good news is that Stardust's temperature hasn't gone up any more. That's a good sign, Ash." He checked his watch. "Dr. Frankel won't be here for another couple of hours. We'll keep an eye on Stardust. Why don't you run up to the house and have breakfast and maybe catch a little sleep? I'm sure you didn't get much last night."

Ashleigh gave Stardust a hug and headed for the house. Her father seemed to think that things were going to turn out okay, but Ashleigh had a feeling that Stardust and her unborn foal weren't out of danger yet.

11

The crunch of tires on gravel invaded Ashleigh's dreamless sleep. She sat up slowly, swinging her feet over the side of the bed, and rubbed her eyes. Peeking through the blinds, she spotted Dr. Frankel's truck easing up to the barn. The kindly vet climbed out of his vehicle and opened the truck's canopy, shoving medicines and bandages into the pockets of his blue veterinary coveralls.

Ashleigh scrambled for her clothes. She wanted to be there when the vet got to Stardust. She pulled on her jeans and slipped her arms into the first shirt she grabbed from the closet.

She pounded down the stairs and out the back door. Her parents were just leading the vet to see Stardust when she reached the pen. "How is she?" Ashleigh asked her parents, trying not to let her voice betray just how worried she was.

Mrs. Griffen opened the gate for everyone to enter. "There's been no change from when you left her a few hours ago, Ash."

Ashleigh went in first, breathing a relieved sigh when she saw Stardust on her feet, her belly still rounded with the coming foal. She waited and watched while Dr. Frankel took Stardust's temperature and listened to her insides with the stethoscope.

Ashleigh counted the ants marching across the dirt by the water trough while she waited for the vet to speak.

After what felt like eons, Dr. Frankel pulled the stethoscope from his ears and turned to the Griffens. "Her temperature is still one-oh-three-point-five, but all of her gut sounds are normal, considering how sick she is. I'd say you should just keep doing what you've been doing and wait for her to show signs of improvement," he advised.

Dr. Frankel pointed to the trash can next to the big barn. "You need to keep all of this dirty bedding and anything you use on Stardust separate so it can be burned or disposed of properly," he said. "All of this stuff is contaminated, and it will be more contagious after those nodules under her jaw break. You need to get rid of the dirty bedding and rags immediately so that none of the other horses is exposed."

"What about the foal?" Ashleigh asked, unable to stand the wait any longer.

Dr. Frankel ran his hand along Stardust's side. "So far everything seems to be okay," he said. "Just keep a watch on her temperature to make sure it doesn't go up another degree. If it does, give me an emergency call. With some luck the fever will break soon."

Ashleigh stayed behind in the stall while her parents and Dr. Frankel went to tend the sick yearlings and to check several of the broodmares that were ready to foal.

She began the same routine of the night before, alternating between sponging the mare's hot body and giving small amounts of water at a time with the drench gun to help keep Stardust hydrated. When Stardust was sleeping, Ashleigh helped her parents with the daily chores.

When Emily got home from school that day, she went straight to Stardust's stall. "How is she?" she asked as she handed Ashleigh their homework assignments.

Ashleigh shrugged. "I haven't really seen any improvement, but she hasn't gotten any worse, so I guess that's good."

"I'll do your afternoon chores for you so you can spend more time with Stardust," Emily volunteered.

Ashleigh smiled her thanks. She could tell Emily was truly sorry for what had happened.

In the evening the nodules under Stardust's chin broke and drained. Ashleigh spent a lot of time cleaning the sores and disposing of the contaminated rags. She was glad that the sickness had been limited to just the three horses. She couldn't imagine what it would be like if all the horses became sick. She'd heard horror stories of entire broodmare barns and racing stables that had been wiped out by a disease.

At feeding time that night, Ashleigh took Stardust's temperature again. She was pleasantly surprised to see that it had gone down by a half a degree. She waited until suppertime to take it again, but Stardust's temperature hovered around 103 degrees and wouldn't drop any lower.

Stardust seemed to be breathing a little easier, but she still refused to eat. Ashleigh tried to tempt the mare with a sweet feed mash, but Stardust only sniffed it and turned away. "Come on, Stardust," Ashleigh pleaded. "You've got to eat something. You're always such a greedy gut. Can't you take just a few bites of your hay or grain?"

The mare remained where she was with her head hung low, seemingly oblivious to everything except her own misery.

After supper that night, Ashleigh was readying her things for the barn when her mother entered her bedroom.

"Would you like me to keep watch over Stardust tonight so you can get some sleep?" Mrs. Griffen offered.

Ashleigh shook her head. "I want to do it, Mom. Stardust and her foal need me. I think she's more comfortable when I'm there. She knows me best."

Mrs. Griffen handed her a pair of fuzzy socks from the drawer. "I'm sure you're probably right about that, Ash, but you need your sleep. Your father and I think you should go to school tomorrow."

Ashleigh looked up in surprise. "But Stardust isn't better yet. I've got to stay with her! What if something happens while I'm at school?"

Mrs. Griffen smiled. "Ashleigh, your father and I have been taking care of horses since before you were born. I'm sure we can take care of Stardust to your satisfaction while you're at school."

Ashleigh looked down at the bedspread, picking at imaginary lint. "I'm sorry," she said softly. "I didn't mean that you and Dad didn't know how to take care of Stardust."

Mrs. Griffen ruffled her hair. "You can sleep in the barn tonight, Ash, but tomorrow you have to go to school, so try to get some sleep. Stardust will be just fine."

Ashleigh gathered her things. Emily was still in the bathroom taking a bath, so she said good night to her cousin through the door. She looked in on Rory and Caroline before going downstairs.

Ashleigh couldn't hold back a smile when she saw

Caroline's movie star magazines and nail polish fighting for space on the dresser beside Rory's horse books and toy cars. "How's it going?" she asked.

Rory was already asleep in his temporary roll-away bed, but Caroline was up doing some last-minute homework. Her papers were spread all over Rory's twin bed.

"It gets a little cramped in here sometimes," Caroline said. "But Rory and I are getting along fine. How's Stardust doing?"

Ashleigh shrugged. "She's still about the same, but Dr. Frankel thinks that her foal will be okay if her temperature doesn't go up. It actually dropped a half a degree."

"That's great, Ash," Caroline said. "I'm sure everything's going to work out fine. That baby will be born before long, and you'll be spoiling it rotten."

Ashleigh smiled at the image of Stardust and her foal. "Thanks, Caro," she said as she backed out of the room. "I'll see you in the morning."

Ashleigh left the house and got settled in for the night in Stardust's stall. Just as she was shaking out her sleeping bag, she heard the sound of footsteps outside.

"Ash?"

It was Emily's voice. "I'm here. Come on in, Em," Ashleigh said.

Emily stepped into the stall with a plate of cookies

and two glasses of milk. "I thought you might want a snack before you go to bed."

"I won't be going to sleep for a while," Ashleigh said as she grabbed a chocolate chip cookie and took a big swig of the milk. "I've got to try to get some more water into Stardust, and I need to clean her nostrils. She's not sweating right now, so I probably won't have to give her a sponge bath."

"Could I stay and help?" Emily asked hopefully.

Ashleigh nodded. "Sure, Em. You can help me give her some water and get her settled in for the night."

Stardust accepted their ministrations with patience. When she got tired, she lay down in the straw, buckling her legs with a grunt as she nestled into the deep bedding.

Ashleigh and Emily sat in the corner watching as the little mare breathed heavily, wheezing with each labored breath.

"Look!" Emily said, pointing to Stardust's belly. "I think I saw the foal kick."

Ashleigh slowly sat up on her knees, trying not to startle Stardust and cause her to get up. "I don't see it," she said, concentrating hard in the dim light of the stall.

"There it is again!" Emily said excitedly.

Ashleigh felt her heart thump against her ribs. "I

see!" she whispered, inching forward to get a better view.

Emily looked to Ashleigh. "That's a good sign, isn't it?"

Ashleigh pursed her lips. "I'm not sure. But if the baby's moving, that means it's still alive, and that's got to be good!" she said.

They watched for several more minutes. The unborn foal moved three more times, its little legs beating a tattoo on Stardust's sides as it shifted into a different position. After another ten minutes, they gave up looking.

Emily gathered the empty glasses and cookie plate. "I'd better get to bed. I'll stop by first thing in the morning."

"Thanks for bringing the snack," Ashleigh said. "I'll see you at breakfast."

Once Emily left, Ashleigh ignored the cot and settled into the corner of the stall. It was early spring and the nights were still cold, but she had on her thick sweatshirt, so she was comfortable.

She watered Stardust several more times and sponge-bathed her sometime after midnight. The last thing she remembered before drifting off to sleep was that Stardust seemed to be resting more comfortably than she had since she got sick.

Ashleigh woke when Jonas shook her arm at feeding time the next morning. She jumped and looked around the stall for Stardust.

"She's outside," Jonas said. "I've already taken her temperature, and it's down." He smiled broadly. "I think this little girl's ready to kick this thing now."

Ashleigh hopped up and dusted the straw from her clothing, then went out to see her mare. Jonas was right, she thought. Stardust still looked ill, but she seemed to be stronger now. She even took a sip from the drinking trough.

Jonas handed Ashleigh a bucket. "Why don't you see if you can coax her into eating some of her grain?" he suggested.

Ashleigh took the bucket and picked out a handful of oats. "Here you go, girl. You love this stuff."

Stardust pricked her ears and showed an interest in the food, but she only lipped a few kernels from Ashleigh's hand, chewing them slowly before blowing through her lips and coughing.

"I've got to go to school today," Ashleigh told Jonas. "Can you help my parents keep a good eye on Stardust? I'll be right home after school."

Jonas nodded. "You'd better get up to the house and get something to eat. I'll finish up here."

Ashleigh gave Stardust a big hug, promising to be back to tend to her as soon as she could. Then she went to the house to get ready for school. She barely had enough time to slug down some cold cereal before Caroline herded them all out the door to the bus stop.

Mona was waiting for them, and Ashleigh filled her in on all the details of the past forty-eight hours.

Mona handed Ashleigh an extra doughnut she had brought. "I'm glad to hear she's doing a little better," she said as she licked the powdered sugar off her fingers. "Jamie and Lynne told me that a stable across town has lost a couple of horses to some new sickness that's going around. I'm being really careful with Frisky. I don't know what I'd do if anything happened to her."

The bus arrived, and they all climbed aboard. Emily let Ashleigh sit with Mona so that she could finish her story. Too soon they arrived at school and made their way to their first class.

Ashleigh had a horrible day at school. She spent every minute of it thinking about Stardust and wondering how she was doing. She called home at lunchtime, but no one answered the phone. That worried her, and she spent the rest of the day thinking of all the horrible things that could be happening back at Edgardale. With her mind so occupied, she flunked several pop quizzes and didn't finish her assignment for reading. By the time they got onto the bus at the end of the day, she was a nervous wreck.

"Calm down, Ash!" Mona said as the bus screeched to a halt at their stop. "I'm sure everything is just fine. I'll go with you."

They got off the bus, and all three girls trotted up the driveway, their backpacks flopping rhythmically against their shoulder blades as they jogged to the stallion pen where Stardust was being stabled.

Stardust was standing out in the sunshine, nibbling daintily on a hay net that had been tied to the fence.

Ashleigh grinned so wide, it hurt. Stardust was eating again—that meant she was getting better. Things were finally looking up!

12

Ashleigh was just feeding carrots to Stardust and marveling at her recovery when she heard a car coming up the driveway. A moment later the door to the house banged open and Rory flew across the porch.

"Emily, your mother is here to visit!" Rory called as he flew out to meet his aunt Gayle.

Ashleigh gave Stardust a pat and squeezed between the fence boards, running to greet her aunt as the car stopped in front of the house. She spotted Emily as her cousin rounded the side of the house and raced over to hug her mother.

Mrs. Griffen came down the steps and handed her sister a cup of coffee, then motioned her into the house. "We're just getting ready to go work with your yearlings," she said.

Emily took her mother's hand, swinging it happily.

"You should see our yearlings now!" she said excitedly. "Especially Midnight Flyer. He's so beautiful!"

Aunt Gayle smiled and hugged Emily again. "Your father really wanted to make this trip, but he's still too weak. The doctors feel that he should be back to normal in another month, and then you can come back home." She ran a loving hand over Emily's hair. "You don't know how much we've missed you."

Mrs. Griffen offered a plate of Danish to her sister. "Emily misses you, too," she said. "She has a lot of fun playing with the kids, but every now and then she gets that sad look on her face." She winked at Emily, who sat next to her mother looking embarrassed that she was the topic of discussion.

"Let's go see the horses!" Emily said as she stuffed a big bite of sweet pastry into her mouth. "Ashleigh has taught me so much, and I'm even riding Stardust now." She paused. "Well, not since she's gotten sick, but I'm really riding again, Mom!"

They finished the plate of pastries and filed out to the barn. Mr. Griffen and Jonas already had the colts and fillies haltered and ready for some lessons. "Good to see you, Gayle," Mr. Griffen said with a welcoming wave. "We'll be loading these yearlings into the trailer just as soon as the girls get them brushed. It's important for horses to be able to load and unload well, but this bunch is going to need a lot more practice," he said with a laugh.

Ashleigh handed Emily her brush bucket and they got busy grooming the horses. Ashleigh was proud of the way Emily handled the yearlings now. Some of her fear seemed to be gone, and she looked happy to be performing for her mother.

"You're really riding again?" Emily's mother asked.

Emily finished picking out the bay colt's hooves and stood, dusting the dirt from her hands. "I'm still pretty scared when I'm up there," she admitted as she pulled a soft body brush from the bucket. "We don't do anything more than walk right now, but I'm getting better." She stared off into the distance with a wistful look on her face. "Someday I'm going to be able to gallop again."

Aunt Gayle walked down the line of yearlings, patting each one and speaking softly to them. She turned to the Griffens. "They look great, guys!" She ran a finger beneath her eyes and wiped away a tear. "I really don't know what Robert and I would have done if it weren't for you."

Mrs. Griffen stepped forward and gave her sister a big hug. "That's what families are for."

Just then Justin, who had offered to help load the yearlings, rode up on Jocko. Introductions were made while he turned his horse loose in an empty paddock.

Mr. Griffen smiled and shook the boy's hand. "We can always use a good horseman," he said. "Your parents have trained you well."

Ashleigh thought Justin looked pleased with the compliment, but her father was right—Justin was good with the horses. She was glad they had become friends.

Ashleigh and Justin led the young animals two at a time to the horse trailer and handed them to the adults to load. Emily was even able to lead the gray filly and stand with her quietly while she was awaiting her turn to be put in the trailer.

"You're doing great, Emily," Ashleigh said encouragingly. "By the time you go home you'll be ready to help your parents tend to all the horses again."

Emily fiddled with the lead rope, twisting it around in her hands, and stared at the ground. "I just wish I weren't such a scaredy-cat when it comes to riding," she said in a low voice. "I wish Stardust were better so I could start riding again."

Ashleigh handed her colt off to her father. "Justin has offered to let us use Jocko," Ashleigh said. "We'll probably have to get you started on him. Stardust is too close to foaling now to be carrying a rider, especially after this illness."

Emily's head snapped up. "Oh, no," she said with her eyes wide. "I couldn't ride Jocko. He's too much horse for me."

"Then maybe we should get you started on Moe," Ashleigh suggested. She almost laughed at the comical look on her cousin's face.

"Moe's a pony," Emily said with disdain. "I'm too big for him."

Ashleigh shrugged. "I still ride Moe when Rory lets me. Look at it this way," she said with a grin. "You won't have far to fall if you come off."

Ashleigh could tell by the look on her cousin's face that Emily wasn't amused. She sighed and went back to get another yearling to load. If Emily wanted to ride again, she'd have to pick either Jocko or Moe. Mona had offered to let Emily ride Frisky, but Frisky was pure Thoroughbred and had a lot more energy than Justin's horse. Emily would have to make a choice.

A week later, Ashleigh sighed as she peered out the window through the gray drizzle to where the yearlings were huddled under the shelter in their paddock. She frowned at the large puddles that had formed everywhere around the farm. It had been raining nonstop for two days, and the weather forecaster had reported that the entire week was supposed to be filled with clouds and showers. Already the streams were rising, and there was talk of flooding if the rain continued the way it had been.

The rain was bad enough, but with the heat of summer coming, there were also terrible lightning storms. Ashleigh and Emily had spent hours in the barn, trying to calm the frightened horses when the thunder rolled.

Two more foals had been born at Edgardale over the last several days. Ashleigh couldn't wait to get home from school each day so she could play with them. Stardust was only two weeks away from her due date now, and she was almost as big as the barn.

Even though Stardust had barely begun to bag up with milk, Ashleigh's father had officially put her on foal watch, commenting that mares could safely foal up to two weeks on either side of their due date. And Ashleigh knew that with a mare that had never foaled before, anything could happen.

She felt her heart jump at the thought of the coming foal. She had gone through so much with Stardust during the mare's illness, she could hardly believe they had actually made it to foal watch!

Emily leaned across from her bed and smacked Ashleigh with a pillow. "Are you thinking about that foal again?"

Ashleigh closed the curtain and nodded. "That's just about all I think about these days."

Emily drew her knees up and rested her chin on them. "I talked to my mom and dad last night, and they said we've got five foals on the ground right now." She smiled dreamily. "They say one of them looks just like Midnight Flyer."

Ashleigh whacked Emily with her own pillow. "Now

look who's daydreaming!" She ducked as another pillow came flying her way. "Nice try," she yelled with a laugh as she ran to the door. "Come on, Em. We've got to go do our barn chores before dinner."

Ashleigh put on her rain slicker and pulled up the hood before stepping out into the steady drizzle. She could hear a low rumble in the distance and knew that a thunderstorm was on the way. She and Emily ran all the way to the barn, splashing in the deep puddles that had formed in the low spots. She pulled open the heavy barn door, leaning into it with all her might as a strong wind caught it and tried to pull it off its runners. It took both her and Emily to close the door.

Jonas handed them a bunch of hay nets to fill. "Looks like another wet one tonight," he observed. "If this rain doesn't stop soon, we're going to have to move some horses around. That big puddle at the end of the barn is almost ready to seep into the far stall."

Ashleigh was glad that Stardust was safely nestled in her dry stall at the opposite end of the barn. She filled her mare's hay net with sweet-smelling timothy and went to hang it in her stall.

"How are you doing, girl?" Ashleigh said as she stood on a bucket to tie the hay net to its ring on the wall. She laughed as Stardust took a big, hungry bite from the hay, ripping the hay net out of her hands before she had a chance to get it tied. "All right," she said in mock anger as she stooped to pick up the hay net and shooed the mare to the corner of the stall. "Now you can wait until I get it tied before you get to eat any of it."

She quickly strung the hay net and stood back to watch Stardust tear at the hay. She couldn't believe that Stardust was so healthy now; not long before, Ashleigh had been worried that she might lose both Stardust and her foal. She ran a hand over the mare's big belly, smiling when she felt a slight movement near her flank. "It won't be long now," she whispered. "Everything's finally going the way it's supposed to!"

Ashleigh helped Emily and Caroline with the last few stalls, and then they bundled up for the run back to the house.

"Just a minute," Emily said as she turned back to the tack room. "I forgot to give Stardust her extra helping of carrots."

Ashleigh smiled. She no longer felt jealous about Emily giving Stardust special treatment. She realized that her cousin needed to have a special relationship with a horse to help her get over her fear.

She waited for Emily, and then the two of them ran through the rain toward the warm, dry house. It was Friday night, and Ashleigh could smell the delicious aroma of freshly delivered pizza when they entered the door. She quickly shucked off her jacket and went to help her mother fill the glasses with cold soda.

They had just gathered around the television with their TV trays to watch a movie when there was a loud clap of thunder and the lights flickered. Ashleigh had just enough time to glance at the others in the room before the lights went out completely.

For a few moments they sat in complete darkness, the room coming to light only when there was a flicker of lightning.

Finally Mrs. Griffen lit a candle and brought it into the room. "Looks like we'll be dining by candlelight tonight," she said as she lit several more candles around the living room.

They finished their pizza and pulled out a board game to pass the rest of the time before bed. Emily won the first two games, and Caroline and Ashleigh won one apiece. Rory was pouting pathetically, so they let him win the last two.

When they were finished, Ashleigh got her raincoat from the coatrack and shoved her arms into the sleeves.

Mrs. Griffen stopped her. "You're not going out in this again, Ash."

Ashleigh was surprised. "But I always do a last-minute check of the barn," she protested. "I want to make sure Stardust is okay."

Mr. Griffen helped her back out of the raincoat. "Jonas will keep an eye on her. You stay here, where it's warm and dry."

Ashleigh frowned as she trudged up the stairs to her room. She knew Stardust would be nervous with the storm raging. Ashleigh decided to wait until everyone was asleep, then she'd sneak out to check on her mare.

She grabbed her pajamas and changed in the bathroom, then quickly brushed her teeth. A few minutes later she crawled into bed, waiting for Emily to doze off and the rest of the family to fall asleep.

Ashleigh started thinking about Stardust's coming foal while she listened for all to become quiet downstairs. Her eyes began to grow heavy and she fought to stay awake, but she couldn't resist the pull of sleep.

A large clap of thunder brought her upright in her bed some time later. Ashleigh rubbed her eyes and stared at the clock on her bedside table. It was still off. The power hadn't yet been restored. She cocked her head, thinking she heard the distant sound of a whinny, but it was lost in the heavy rumble of thunder.

She heard another neigh in the night and swung her legs over the side of the bed, reaching for her boots in the darkness. She didn't bother changing out of her pajamas. The raincoat would cover her from head to foot, and her parents would never know she had slipped out in the middle of the night to check the horses.

Ashleigh tiptoed down the stairs and grabbed her raincoat, careful to open the back door with a minimum of squealing from the hinges. The rain came down in sheets as she ran toward the barn, soaking her even through her raincoat. A strong gust of wind almost knocked her off her feet.

Ashleigh slowed as she approached the barn. She heard several worried nickers coming from inside. She stumbled across something lying in her path and almost fell to the muddy ground. A brilliant flash of lightning illuminated the barnyard, giving Ashleigh a look at what she had tripped over. It was the barn door! The heavy winds must have blown it off its hinges.

She entered the dark barn, fumbling for a flashlight that they always kept near the door. She found it and flipped the switch, sending a thin beam of light into the dark barn.

Ashleigh shone the light down the aisle. Her heart slammed into her rib cage as the meager beam cut across the barn aisle, illuminating a stall door that stood open. She hurried into the barn on shaking legs, knowing without having to look that the stall belonged to Stardust.

Her hands were shaking so badly by the time she got to the stall that she could barely hold on to the flashlight. Ashleigh held her breath and pointed the beam into the stall. All the air rushed from her lungs as she sank to the ground on rubber legs.

The stall was empty. Stardust was gone!

13

Ashleigh ran to Jonas's apartment over the barn office and knocked loudly on his door. She could hear him moving about in the darkness as he shuffled to meet her. She tried to get control of her breathing so she would be able to speak, but she felt as though she had just run the Kentucky Derby. The pounding of her heart almost drowned out the sound of the wind howling around the barn.

Jonas finally opened the door. His brow wrinkled in concern when he saw Ashleigh standing there at such a late hour. "What's the matter, Ashleigh?" Jonas asked as he ran a hand through his mussed hair.

"Stardust is missing!" Ashleigh cried. "I've got to run and tell my parents. Could you please start looking for her?"

Jonas rubbed his eyes, trying to shake off the sleep. "What happened?" he asked in a groggy voice.

Ashleigh tried to think. She had to bite her lip to keep from crying. "Emily was the last one in Stardust's stall," she said. "I think she might have left the door open."

Jonas sighed and reached for his jacket and a flashlight, then stepped into the cool darkness of the barn. "I'll check around the stable area. You go wake your parents."

Ashleigh carefully made her way out of the dark barn. She called to Stardust several times but got no answering neigh. The lightning flashed around her as she ran as fast as she could to the house.

She heard Emily's voice from the top of the staircase as she entered the house.

"What's the matter, Ashleigh?" she asked in a quiet voice. "Why are you out in the storm?"

Ashleigh stood at the bottom of the stairs, shining her flashlight up at Emily. So many emotions warred within her—fear, anger, but sadness, too. Emily had made so much progress. How could she have backslid and done something this stupid?

Ashleigh had tried to be patient and forgiving about all of Emily's problems, but this time Stardust and her unborn foal might be in serious trouble.

A loud crack of thunder shook the house and seemed to break loose Ashleigh's anger. "You left Stardust's stall unlocked!" Ashleigh shouted, not car-ing that she was hollering loud enough to wake the entire house.

Emily shook her head, her sleep-tangled hair swinging wildly about her face as she denied the charges. "You're wrong, Ashleigh. I checked the latch twice to make sure it was closed. I'm sure of it!"

Mrs. Griffen came out of her room in her nightgown. "What's going on out here?" She looked from Ashleigh to Emily.

Another flash of lightning lit the room, showing Caroline and Rory standing at the top of the stairs with Emily. Rory rubbed his eyes and yawned. Caroline looked to Ashleigh for an explanation.

Ashleigh pressed her lips in a hard line and pointed an accusing finger at her cousin. "Emily left Stardust's stall door unlatched, and now Stardust is gone! She could be badly hurt."

Mr. Griffen entered the living room, wrapping his robe about him. He scratched the stubble on his chin. "She's got to be in the barn, Ash. We closed all the doors."

"The barn door blew off," Ashleigh said. "We've got to go *now*. Stardust could be out there having her foal in this storm!"

Emily cried out from the top of the stairs, "I didn't do it, Ash! You've got to believe me!" she pleaded as tears began to roll down her pale cheeks. "I double-checked the latch before I left. It's not my fault that

Stardust is gone! Something must have happened!"

Ashleigh gave her cousin a look that told Emily she didn't believe a word the girl said.

"All right, girls, that's enough for now," Mr. Griffen said. "Tomorrow we'll look into the matter and find out what happened. In the meantime, Caroline can stay with Rory, and the rest of us will get dressed and check the barnyard for Stardust."

Rory wiped the sleep from his eyes. "I want to look for Stardust, too," he whined.

Mrs. Griffen motioned for Caroline to take the sleepy little boy back into his room. "It's too dangerous out there right now, Rory. You can help when it's light out."

Ashleigh left to find Jonas while the others were getting dressed. She crossed her fingers, hoping that the old groom would have Stardust safely back in her stall by the time she reached the barn, but the mare's stall was still empty. She found Jonas outside the barn looking for hoofprints in the mud.

Jonas shone his flashlight on the ground. "These could be your mare's tracks here," he said, pointing to a set of hoofprints that led toward the driveway. "But the rain comes and goes and it's washing the prints away."

Ashleigh tried to keep her fear reined in, but the thought of Stardust leaving the property and crossing the road in the dark made her stomach clench. The fact that the ground was muddy and could be slippery made it even worse.

Ashleigh's parents and Emily arrived, each holding a flashlight. Ashleigh glared at Emily, who met her gaze.

Emily crossed her arms and looked defiantly back at Ashleigh. "I didn't do it, Ashleigh," she said simply. "It's not fair of you to blame me."

Ashleigh tossed her hands in the air. "You were the last one in the stall, Em! Look at all of the other mistakes you've made," she shouted. "Why should I believe you?"

Jonas interrupted. "Because Emily didn't do it," he said as he stood and wiped his muddy hands on his coveralls.

All eyes turned to the old stable hand. "What do you mean?" Ashleigh asked.

Jonas pulled his hat lower as the rain began to fall. A jagged flash of lightning cut across the dark sky, illuminating his weathered face. "The latch on Stardust's stall was broken. She must have panicked at one of the loud claps of thunder and lunged against the door," he explained.

Ashleigh's mouth dropped open. "Are you sure?" she said as she glanced at Emily, feeling a hot blush creep up her cheeks. She felt horribly ashamed of herself for blaming her cousin before she had proof.

Jonas nodded. "The latch is ripped right off the door."

Ashleigh turned to Emily. She swallowed hard. "Um . . . I'm really sorry, Em. Will you forgive me?"

Emily shook her head and sighed. She looked angry, but there was something else in her eyes, too—something more like sadness. "I don't know, Ash," she said quietly. "I've tried so hard to do what you say and to be like you, but sometimes you treat me really badly."

Mr. Griffen broke into the argument. "All right, girls. This isn't helping us find Stardust. We'll talk about it later. I want everyone to spread out and check the immediate area. We'll meet back here in a few minutes."

Ashleigh tried to meet Emily's gaze, but her cousin turned and walked in the opposite direction. Ashleigh couldn't tell if Emily was crying or the wetness on her cheeks was raindrops, but Emily's shoulders were slumped, and Ashleigh had the feeling that her cousin wasn't feeling as brave as she had seemed a few moments ago.

Ashleigh pointed her flashlight down the driveway and went in search of her mare. She'd have to find a way to make it up to Emily later.

Twenty minutes later, when everyone met back at the barn, no one had seen any sign of Stardust.

"I think she got out on the road," Ashleigh said, flinching when another loud clap of thunder rolled overhead. "We need to go out and look for her."

Mrs. Griffen shook her head. "It's too dangerous, Ash. There are trees down and some power lines are hanging. I think we should wait until daylight."

"But Mom—" Ashleigh began.

Mr. Griffen put a fatherly hand on Ashleigh's shoulder. "Look, honey, we know how much Stardust means to you, but you girls mean even more to us. It's too dangerous out here in the dark with this storm raging," he said. "We'll get started at first light."

Ashleigh opened her mouth to protest, but her father would hear no argument.

"Up to the house, girls," Mr. Griffen ordered as he herded them toward the big white farmhouse. "The sun will be up in a few hours. We'll look for her at first light."

Emily sprinted ahead, but Ashleigh plodded slowly toward the house, straining her ears and eyes for any hint of Stardust that might change her father's mind and let her continue the search.

The lightning flashed again, so bright that for a fraction of a second it seemed like daylight. Ashleigh scanned the grounds, hoping to see motion that might indicate a horse, but the trees were swaying so wildly from the high winds that it was hard to detect any other movement. She called Stardust's name one last time before entering the house. A gust of wind carried the cry, but there was no answering whinny in return.

She opened the door to the house with a heavy

heart. Stardust was out in the storm, ready to foal, and there wasn't anything she could do at the moment. She could only hope the mare had found a safe shelter someplace and that she wasn't foaling. Ashleigh knew that anything could happen with a first foal. Some mares even died giving birth.

Ashleigh sighed and tried to push that thought far from her mind. Stardust was going to be okay. She just had to be!

She peeled off her raincoat, trying to avoid her parents' sympathetic looks. They couldn't bring Stardust back, either. But when Mrs. Griffen opened her arms to her daughter, Ashleigh ran into them, letting loose the torrent of tears she had been holding back.

"It's going to be okay, Ash," Mrs. Griffen crooned. "We'll find Stardust in the morning. She'll be fine."

Ashleigh cried until she had no more tears left, then kissed her parents good night and went to her room. She knew she wouldn't sleep a wink, but she'd have to be in bed to satisfy her parents.

When Ashleigh opened the door to her room, she heard Emily's soft sobs, and she felt even worse. Her cousin was huddled under the covers of her own bed with her back facing the door and her shoulders shaking. Ashleigh moved to the other side of the room to get into her bed. Emily turned over so that her back was to Ashleigh once again.

Ashleigh bit her lip. She really did owe her cousin an apology. She walked to the side of Emily's bed and sat down on it. "Em?" she whispered.

"Go away," Emily whimpered, pulling the covers over her head.

Ashleigh took a deep breath, letting it out slowly as she tried to find the right words. "Look, Em," she began. "There's no way I can make this right. I was really stupid to blame you without even finding out the facts. I was just really upset and you were the closest one to take it out on. It was wrong of me, and if you never want to speak to me again, I'll understand. I'm just so worried about Stardust."

Ashleigh took a deep breath, trying to stop the tears from coming back, but it didn't work. She went to her own bed and got in, pulling the covers up around her neck and curling into a ball. She cried into her pillow, hoping that no one else could hear. She felt just plain miserable, right down to her bones.

"Ashleigh?" Emily's soft voice echoed in the dark room.

Ashleigh shoved her face farther into her pillow.

"It's okay, Ash," Emily said softly. "I understand. If I had a horse like Stardust, I'd be really worried, too. And I *have* made a lot of mistakes," she admitted. "I can see why you thought it was my fault." Emily paused for a moment. "We're cousins, Ash. We're not supposed to fight like this. Let's just go to sleep now, and we'll get up in a few hours and find your mare together."

Emily's speech made Ashleigh cry even harder. "Okay," she choked out, giving her cousin a grateful look. Then she cried until her throat was dry and sore. By the time she was done, she was so exhausted she couldn't fight the pull of sleep any longer. Her puffy eyes grew heavy as she tried not to let them close. Sometime just before dawn, Ashleigh lost the battle and drifted into a deep, troubled sleep.

She was awakened by a rough shake a short time later. She rolled over and rubbed her eyes, looking into the concerned face of her mother.

"Where's Emily?" Mrs. Griffen asked.

Ashleigh sat up, trying to shake the sleep from her tired mind. "Maybe she's out with the horses?" she said.

Mrs. Griffen shook her head. "We just got back from the barn. Emily's not in the house, and Jonas hasn't seen her."

Ashleigh was fully awake now. She stared at the empty bed next to her. The wind was still howling around the sides of the house, causing the tree branches to whip the outside of her bedroom wall. Her stomach tightened as a foreboding chill crept over her. Now both Emily *and* Stardust were missing in the storm.

14

Ashleigh dressed as quickly as she could. *Has Emily run away?* She slipped on a pair of jeans and grabbed a thick sweatshirt from her drawer. No, that was impossible. She had been so sincere the night before, when she had assured Ashleigh that they would find Stardust together.

Did Emily go out on her own to look for Stardust?

Ashleigh ran down the stairs and grabbed a doughnut off the counter. "I'm going to call Mona's house and see if she's seen Emily."

"It's awfully early to be calling the Gardners," Mr. Griffen said.

Ashleigh dialed the number. "Mona will understand," she said. "I'm sure she'll want to help us." Ashleigh counted the rings as she waited for someone to answer at the other end.

"Hello?"

The voice on the other end was so rough-sounding that Ashleigh almost hung up, thinking that she had dialed the wrong number. "Mona?" Ashleigh said in surprise.

Mona coughed several times and spoke in a strained voice. "I've got a really bad cold, Ash. My mom won't even let me get out of bed. Emily had to go saddle Frisky by herself."

"Emily borrowed Frisky?" Ashleigh was so surprised, she almost dropped the phone. Emily couldn't even ride Stardust without someone walking with her. What made her think she could ride Frisky in a storm?

"Did Emily find Stardust?" Mona asked.

Ashleigh frowned. "We don't even know where Emily is," she admitted. There was a long pause on the end of the line, and Ashleigh began to wonder if Mona had fallen back asleep or hung up.

Mona's voice finally came over the phone line with a quiver. "Emily wanted to borrow Frisky because she's best friends with Stardust. Emily thought she could find Stardust if Frisky would call to her. But I thought you guys knew where she was going," Mona said. "What if they're hurt?"

"Don't worry, Mona," Ashleigh assured her friend. "I won't let anything happen to either of them. I'll be over in a few minutes to check for hoofprints. Maybe I'll be able to tell which direction they went."

"I wish I could help," Mona said in a miserable voice. "Be careful, Ash. The wind is still blowing pretty hard."

Ashleigh said goodbye and hung up the phone. Emily probably had at least an hour's head start. She told her parents what Mona had said as she pulled on her rubber boots and raincoat.

"Wait for us at the Gardners' place," Mrs. Griffen said. "We'll figure out what to do from there."

Ashleigh cut across the property, heading toward the Gardners' fence line. It began to drizzle again, so she pulled up her hood as she jogged along, trying to avoid the deep puddles that had gathered in the fields.

Mona waved to her from her bedroom window. Ashleigh went around back, where Emily would have saddled Frisky, to see if she could find any clues. She saw the prints leading from the mounting block. The marks ambled right and left, as if Emily had been having trouble steering the mare.

Ashleigh followed the tracks across the Gardners' front lawn. When they reached the road, a small pair of boot prints appeared beside the horse tracks. Ashleigh studied the prints, which were becoming less obvious now that the rain was coming down harder. Emily must have gotten scared and dismounted.

She stared back toward Edgardale. Her parents had told her to wait for them, but if she waited, the rain might wash away all the tracks. She crammed her hands deep into her raincoat pockets and looked down the driveway, willing her parents to appear in the car. After a few minutes she decided she couldn't wait any longer. She crossed the street to pick up the tracks.

Ashleigh made her way through several large fields. After a while the tracks became less and less evident until she finally lost them in the middle of a flooded hay field.

She wiped the rain from her face and peered through the downpour. The prints seemed to be leading in the direction of Justin's house and the woods that lay behind it.

"Emily!" Ashleigh hollered as loudly as she could. She waited several seconds, straining to hear something besides the constant splatter of rain hitting the standing water in the field and the heavy winds whistling through the trees.

Something sounded in the distance, and Ashleigh cocked her head, not sure if what she'd heard had been a high-pitched whinny or just another sound from the storm. She headed toward the woods where she thought the sound had come from.

Ashleigh was halfway across the waterlogged field when she saw a horse and rider approaching in the distance. Justin! She waited for him to reach her. "How did you know I was here?" she asked when Jocko pulled to a halt, tossing his head in protest at being out in the storm.

"Your parents called my house when you weren't at Mona's house waiting for them. They asked me to help look for you." He leaned down and offered his hand. "Come on, I'll give you a ride back to Edgardale."

Ashleigh stared toward the woods, trying to make a decision. If she went back to Edgardale, she could lose precious time that could mean life or death for her cousin, Stardust, and Frisky. If she didn't go back to Edgardale, she would be in serious trouble.

Another cry came from the direction of the woods, and Ashleigh's head snapped around. Jocko pricked his ears and snorted. "Did you hear that?" Ashleigh asked, wishing that the sound were clearer so she could tell what it was.

Justin shook his head. "I didn't hear anything, but it sure got Jocko's attention." He steadied the reins as the chestnut danced about, flicking his ears in the direction of the sound.

Ashleigh mounted up behind Justin. "We've got to go check that out," she said. "It could be Stardust or Emily and Frisky. They could be in a lot of trouble!"

Justin held Jocko's reins. "But *you're* going to be in a lot of trouble for disobeying your parents if you don't go back," he reminded her.

Ashleigh gave Jocko a nudge with her heels to get

him started. "This is more important," she said. "I'll take my chances with my parents later. If we can find Emily and the horses, maybe my parents will go easy on me," she said hopefully.

She held on to Justin's belt loops as Jocko cantered across the field. The water from his pounding hoofs splattered upward, and Ashleigh could feel the cold water getting up under her rain gear. She was chilled and miserable, but she didn't care. She had to find her cousin and the horses!

"There's something up ahead by the stream," Justin said. "See the way Jocko is pricking his ears?"

Ashleigh stared through the rain. She could see what looked like a horse or a cow in the distance. Jocko raised his head and whinnied, his sides shaking with the force of the greeting. Ashleigh held on tight. It had to be a horse, but which one? Frisky or Stardust?

As they came closer, Ashleigh recognized Frisky's bay coat and four white stockings and spotted Emily hanging on to the reins as Frisky paced up and down the swollen stream, calling to something on the other side. Emily wore a worried expression, but as Ashleigh and Justin approached, Ashleigh could see the relief washing over her cousin's face. Ashleigh slid off Jocko's back and took Frisky's reins from Emily.

"Ashleigh! Oh, thank goodness! I didn't know how much longer I could hold her!" Emily cried through chattering teeth. "Frisky keeps calling to another horse on the other side, and I'm sure it's Stardust. It sounds just like her, but her neigh is very faint." She paused to wipe the tears and rain off of her face. "Frisky wanted to swim the stream and go to her, but I knew she shouldn't. It was so hard to keep her here and not let her go."

Ashleigh stared at the roiling, muddy water, which used to be a small, clear stream. "You did great, Em," she said as she patted her cousin on the back. "Frisky could have been swept away and killed if she'd tried to swim the stream."

Emily looked to Justin and Ashleigh. "What do we do now? I'm sure that's Stardust in the woods. That's why I brought Frisky. I knew she'd find her best friend."

Justin pointed up the way. "There's a bridge up the stream. That's the best way to get to this section of the woods, but it might be under water, and it's not safe for the horses. We'll have to take them back to the barn if we decide to go that way."

"Let's take a look and see if it's passable before we put the horses away," Ashleigh said. She paused and patted Emily on the shoulder. "Great thinking, Em. I wish you'd told me where you were going, but it was smart to use Frisky as our detective." She mounted up on Frisky and waited for Justin to help Emily up behind her. They walked the horses to the bridge.

Ashleigh felt her stomach tighten when she saw the bridge. It was an old wooden structure that the farm's previous owner had built several years ago. She had crossed it many times in quieter weather, and she remembered that there had been many rickety spots and loose boards.

The water was now up to the walkway, lapping at the boards and sometimes spilling over. Small tree branches and pieces of grass and debris caught on the bridge, backing the water up so that some of it spilled around the sides of the structure. If they decided to cross it, they would have to wade through water even to get to the bridge.

Emily looked doubtful. "I don't know . . . ," she murmured.

A desperate neigh cut through the woods, and everyone turned in that direction. Jocko and Frisky answered the panicked call with a shake of their heads.

"That's her!" Ashleigh cried. "That's Stardust!"

Justin wheeled Jocko around. "Let's get these horses back to my barn so we can go find her."

They picked their way back to Justin's house, avoiding the deep mud and large puddles. When they reached the barn, Justin dismounted and handed his reins to Ashleigh. "I'll go to the house and call

Edgardale to let your parents know that you're here, that Emily and Frisky are safe, and that we might have found Stardust," Justin said.

By the time Justin returned from the house, Ashleigh and Emily had the horses unsaddled and rubbed with dry towels. The horses stood in the stalls, happily munching on hay.

"Caroline answered the phone," Justin said as he led the way out of the barn. "Your parents are out looking for you and Emily. She's got to find them."

"What about your parents?" Ashleigh asked as she ran to catch up with Justin's long stride. "Are they going to help us?"

Justin pulled up the hood of his slicker as they stepped out into the rain. "My mom left me a note saying there was a break in the fence and some of our horses got out. They're out rounding up the horses and fixing our fence. I left them a note saying where we would be, but I don't know when they'll be back to get it. We're on our own."

Emily wrung her hands. "Shouldn't we wait for someone to help us?" she asked. "This could be really dangerous, Ashleigh. We could get in a lot of trouble."

Ashleigh shook her head. "You can go back to Edgardale if you want, Emily, but I can't wait. Stardust must be in deep trouble or she would have come to meet the horses when we were at the stream." She paused, not wanting to say the next words. "I hope she's not hurt."

Justin began to jog. "Come on—we've got to get over that bridge before it's too dangerous to cross."

Emily still looked unsure as she ran to catch up. "It looks too dangerous to cross now," she said.

They stopped to catch their breath when they reached the bridge. Ashleigh bent over, putting her hands on her knees as she drew in great gulps of air. She hated to admit it, but Emily was right about the bridge. If her mare weren't in trouble, there was no way she would consider crossing the unstable structure.

"I'll go first," Justin said bravely. "I think we should hold on to each other's belt loops with one hand and keep a tight grip on the rail with the other. That way if one of the planks should break . . ."

Ashleigh felt a shiver go up her spine. Justin didn't need to finish the sentence. They all knew how dangerous the situation was.

Another pathetic neigh sounded in the forest. This one was weaker than the last, and Ashleigh knew that they had to hurry. She followed Justin to the foot of the bridge and hooked her fingers through his belt loops, waiting while Emily did the same behind her. Ashleigh prayed that the bridge would hold.

15

The swift water pooled around her boots as they stepped toward the foot of the bridge, but it was shallow there and the current didn't have much strength.

The bridge groaned as they stepped onto it, causing all three of them to suck in their breath as they paused to see if the bridge would hold. It gave several creaks that could be heard over the gurgling of the rushing water, but the boards held.

"Let's go quickly!" Justin shouted.

Ashleigh nodded, and they splashed over the planks, slipping and sliding on the wet grass and slimy stuff that coated the bridge's walkway. When they reached the other side, they leaped eagerly to the safety of the muddy ground.

Ashleigh's hands and legs were shaking so badly, she wasn't sure they would hold her. One look at her two companions told her that they felt the same way. They paused for just a moment to gather their courage, then turned in the direction they thought the whinnies had come from and stepped into the sodden woods.

Ashleigh winced as a tree branch lashed across her face, leaving a scratch on her cheek. She called to Stardust and heard a weak reply. "She's over this way!" Ashleigh said as she took the lead and cut through a patch of large oak trees.

They came to a small clearing, and Ashleigh's knees went weak again at the sight before her. Stardust was caught in the fencing at a place where the water had backed up from the stream and formed a deep pool.

"Easy, girl," Ashleigh crooned, trying to keep the fear she felt deep inside from coming out in her voice.

Stardust snorted, her eyes rolling in terror. She tried to go to Ashleigh, but she floundered helplessly in the chest-high water.

"It looks as though her leg is caught," Justin said. "One of us will have to steady her while the other one goes underwater to find out what's holding Stardust."

Ashleigh waded into the water, taking Stardust's head in her hands and rubbing the sides of her face comfortingly. "I'll go underwater," she said as she took off her raincoat to get rid of some of the weight.

Emily waded into the water and took hold of

Stardust's mane and forelock to steady her. "We'll keep her still while you find out what's wrong," she said, her teeth beginning to chatter with the cold.

Ashleigh reached down Stardust's front leg as far as she could without putting her head underwater. There were sticks and bugs floating in the muddy water. She didn't want to have to put her head beneath it unless it was absolutely necessary. Her hands closed around the place in the wire fencing where it tightened around the mare's hoof. Ashleigh was thankful that the wire wasn't barbed.

"It's twisted," she said. "I think Stardust put her leg through the fence and then turned. We've got to turn her back in the other direction so I can get her foot out."

Justin removed his belt and handed it to Emily, who looped it around Stardust's neck. "Let me have your belts, too, so I can make a halter for her," he said.

Ashleigh and Emily quickly gave their belts to Justin and waited while he fashioned a makeshift halter for the frightened mare.

Ashleigh ran her hand along Stardust's swollen belly. The mare's stomach felt so cold. Her heart squeezed as she tried to find some sign that the foal was okay, but there were no small thumps along Stardust's belly to show that the unborn foal was alive. "We've got to get her out of here *now*," she said, her voice trembling in fear.

Justin interlaced the belts to form a halter and asked Ashleigh and Emily to stand back while he slowly eased Stardust around in the other direction. When the mare was facing the other way, Ashleigh took a deep breath and ducked under the surface of the water, clawing at the fencing to loosen it from Stardust's leg. After a few seconds her lungs felt like they were ready to burst, but she worked at the fencing, spreading the wire and freeing Stardust's leg. When she was done, she rose to the surface, gasping for breath.

Emily led the shaking mare from the water. When they reached solid ground, Stardust shook the extra moisture from her coat and began to shiver uncontrollably.

"We've got to get her back to your barn as fast as we can," Ashleigh said.

Justin pointed to a trail. "This way is a lot longer than the other, but we can't take Stardust over the bridge."

Ashleigh kept a steadying hand on Stardust as she led the mare along the trail toward Justin's house. Stardust kept shivering and couldn't seem to gain any warmth. They would have to blanket her and call the vet as soon as they got to the barn.

They finally reached the field. They still had a ways to go, but Ashleigh sighed in relief, knowing how close they were to help. She smiled when they rounded

Justin's big farmhouse and saw her parents standing in the driveway, but her smile immediately faded when she noted the worried looks on her parents' faces.

"You're safe!" Mr. and Mrs. Griffen ran to the girls and hugged them close.

Mrs. Griffen ran a finger over the scratch on Ashleigh's face and tsked. "I don't know whether to kiss you girls or ground you for life," she said.

"I think we'll do both," Mr. Griffin said, his face pinched with worry, "but we'll have to think about that later. All you kids seem to be fine, but this mare looks like she's in trouble. We'll discuss how you disobeyed orders some other time."

Ashleigh looked to Emily. Her cousin looked as nervous as she felt. Ashleigh had known they were going to be in a lot of trouble for all of their actions, but Stardust was safe. She was willing to accept the punishment. Now she could only hope that Stardust's foal was going to be okay.

"I'll get our trailer hooked up and take the mare home," Justin's father volunteered.

While they waited for the trailer, Ashleigh and Emily covered Stardust with a thick blanket while Justin went to the house to call Dr. Frankel to Edgardale.

Stardust grunted and her belly twitched as she tensed in pain.

"What's happening?" Ashleigh said in panic. It

looked as though Stardust was beginning to colic.

Mr. Griffen observed the little chestnut. "It could be colic, or it could be the beginning stages of labor," he said.

Ashleigh didn't like the way her father's brow furrowed—as though he knew something bad but didn't want to tell anyone else.

"But I thought mares liked to foal at night," Ashleigh said, running her hand over Stardust's belly to feel the deep tremors.

Mrs. Griffen nodded grimly. "Most of them do. However, it's possible that Stardust has suffered so much trauma that she's losing the foal."

Ashleigh gasped, feeling as though she had been kicked in the stomach. "No!" she cried. "That can't happen! We have to save Stardust's baby!"

Emily took Ashleigh's hand and squeezed it reassuringly. "Stardust and the baby are going to be fine, Ash. We won't let anything happen to them."

Ashleigh tried to give Emily a grateful smile, but she couldn't get her lips to move upward. She just nodded, knowing that Emily would understand.

The trailer pulled up, and they quickly loaded Stardust. Dr. Frankel was waiting for them when they arrived. They immediately put Stardust in her stall. Ashleigh stayed inside with the vet and her father, refusing to leave Stardust's side.

Stardust circled the stall with her head low. She pawed at the bedding and buckled her knees to lie down.

Dr. Frankel got the mare back up and removed her blanket. "I'd like everyone to wait outside," he said as he opened the stall door.

"What's happening?" Ashleigh cried. "I can't leave. Stardust needs me!"

Dr. Frankel nodded. "I think this mare is in labor," he said. "You can stay, Ashleigh. It might make Stardust feel better. Most mares like to deliver by themselves, but Stardust is pretty shaken up from her experience. She might do better with you here. I'll wait outside the stall in case she needs me."

Ashleigh looked from the doctor to her parents, feeling as though her heart were going to explode. *Stardust has to be okay!* She glanced at Emily, and Emily gave her a tiny sympathetic nod, as though she knew exactly how Ashleigh felt.

"I want Emily in here, too," Ashleigh said as she motioned her cousin inside.

Emily hesitated, but Ashleigh held the stall door open. "You're the one who found Stardust," she explained. "You deserve to be here to see her first foal born."

Emily's face broke into a smile, and she hurried into

the stall. "Thanks, Ash. I can't wait to see Stardust's foal!"

Ashleigh curled up in the corner beside Emily, drawing her knees up and wrapping her arms around them. The rest of her family went to the tack room to wait.

Ashleigh gnawed her bottom lip as Stardust paced the stall, grunting and groaning in misery. The chestnut lay down and got up several times.

Emily crowded close. "Is she okay?"

Ashleigh nodded. She knew that mares did this to help position their foal for birth, but she couldn't help worrying that something might be wrong. Stardust had been in the cold water for a long time. Had the baby died during that ordeal?

"Easy, girl," she said in a calming voice, feeling anything but calm on the inside. "You're going to have a beautiful baby."

There was a sound of liquid sloshing as Stardust's water broke, indicating that her time had come. The little mare lay down in the stall and groaned, twisting her head back to her stomach to indicate she was in pain.

After a few minutes Stardust lay flat on her side and began the work of pushing the foal from her body.

Ashleigh heard Emily gasp. She nudged Emily's

shoulder reassuringly, but Ashleigh herself still cringed every time Stardust moaned. She chastised herself for being such a baby. She had been through the birthing process many times before with the other Edgardale mares, but it was different when it was her very own horse!

"I see a hoof!" Ashleigh whispered excitedly. Then Stardust pushed again, and a little pink nose with a white stripe appeared on top of the second small hoof.

Ashleigh choked back a gasp. "Dr. Frankel, the nostrils are still. I don't think it's breathing!" She watched with apprehension as Stardust pushed again and the entire nose came into view.

Dr. Frankel spoke softly from outside the stall door. "Just give her a few moments, Ash. Sometimes foals don't take their first breath until their chest clears the mare. They're still receiving oxygen from the umbilical cord."

Stardust grunted, and the entire head of the foal appeared atop the long front legs. Ashleigh wanted to jump for joy when the tiny pink nostrils twitched to life, opening wide to take a breath.

"The foal's alive!" she cried as quietly as she could so that she wouldn't upset the mare. She grinned at Emily, who was as wide-eyed as Ashleigh herself over the special event.

Stardust rested for a few moments before the last big push that would clear the foal's shoulders from her body. The rest of the birthing would come quickly after that.

Ashleigh watched with tears in her eyes as the tiny chestnut foal came into the world and stretched out on the straw, lifting its head slightly to take in the new surroundings. It looked identical to Stardust.

Dr. Frankel quietly entered the stall and knelt beside the new foal. "It looks like you've got a filly!" he said as he put his stethoscope to the filly's chest. "She's a little weak from the trauma of the cold water, but I think if you girls rub her down good with some warm towels, she'll be up and nursing in no time."

Ashleigh smiled so broadly that she felt as though her cheeks might pop. The rest of the family gathered outside the stall to see the newest addition to Edgardale.

"It's a miracle!" Ashleigh said as she ran her hand over the wet coat of the tiny copper filly, encouraging Emily to do the same. She smiled when the newborn lifted her head and made soft sucking noises.

Stardust nickered a greeting and rolled onto her stomach with her legs tucked under her, resting for a few minutes before she stood to nurse her new foal.

"That's a perfect name for her," Mrs. Griffen said as

she handed Ashleigh and Emily some towels so they could begin drying off the new filly. "I think we should name her Stardust's Miracle!"

Ashleigh stood back as Stardust got to her feet and nuzzled her new filly. Ashleigh helped the teetering foal to stand and nurse, then threw her arms around Stardust's neck. "You did great, girl!" She smiled proudly at mother and baby. "Stardust's Miracle it is!"

She ran her hands over the new filly, staring in wonder as the tiny foal nursed greedily. With Stardust's illness and her trauma in the storm that day, it was truly a miracle that this new filly was standing before them.

She turned to Emily, seeing the same look of awe on her cousin's face. But she also noted a longing in Emily's eyes, and all at once something clicked in Ashleigh's mind. If it hadn't been for Emily, Stardust and her foal might not have returned safely to Edgardale. She had fought her fear of horses to save Stardust—and Stardust's Miracle.

"She's *so* beautiful!" Emily cried as she touched the soft, wispy mane of the newborn. "You're so lucky, Ashleigh."

Ashleigh grinned. "Yes, I *am* lucky," she agreed. "I'm lucky to have such a wonderful mare, and I'm even luckier to have such a great cousin who was willing to risk her own safety to save her. Emily . . ." With a smile,

Ashleigh reached out her hand and touched her cousin's arm. "I want *you* to have Stardust's Miracle," she said.

Emily looked up in surprise, her mouth forming a wide O. "*Me?*" she squeaked.

Ashleigh nodded. "You're ready for a horse of your own, Em. And if it hadn't been for you, both Stardust and her foal might not have made it. I want you to have Miracle."

Emily hugged Ashleigh hard. "Thank you so much!" She pulled back, and Ashleigh could see tears forming at the corners of her cousin's eyes. "I've got six months before Miracle can be weaned," she said. "I'm going to work hard every day to improve my horse skills so that when Miracle comes home to me, I'll be the best horsewoman ever!" She looked at Ashleigh, and her cheeks colored. "That is, except for you, Ashleigh. You'll always be the best. But I'm going to try to be just like you!"

Ashleigh smiled. She knew Emily would keep her word. "Just do me one favor," Ashleigh requested. "It's okay that we're going to have horses that look alike. But promise me that from now on, you'll make sure you're wearing your own choice of clothes."

Everyone laughed as Emily slapped Ashleigh a high five.

Ashleigh threw her arms around Stardust and gave

her mare a big hug. She would miss Miracle when the foal went to live with Emily, but even without the beautiful filly, Ashleigh felt like the luckiest girl in the world. She had the greatest, bravest mare ever in Stardust, a wonderful family, and an amazing life working with the animals she loved. Ashleigh pressed her cheek against Stardust's neck and breathed in her warm, horsy smell.

She hoped this feeling could last forever.